THE TORN WORLD

BOOK FIVE OF
THE HARVESTING SERIES

MELANIE KARSAK

THE TORN WORLD

Clockpunk Press, 2016

Published by Clockpunk Press

ISBN-13: 978-0692775202

ISBN-10: 069277520X

Cover art by Hynds Studio

Editing by Becky Stephens Editing

Proofreading by Contagious Edits

DEDICATION

for Naomi and Brian

THE TORN WORLD

The undead closed in.

I closed my eyes.

Tristan took me gently by the arm. "Time to go," he whispered.

I nodded, turned, and followed behind him, entering the cave.

Sweet wind blew from the cave. The scent of flowers, and summer, and sunlight perfumed the breeze. I closed my eyes and soaked it in, expecting the rushing feeling I'd experienced the last time, and braced myself for what would come next. In a single instant, before I was swept away, I opened my eyes and looked back at the forest.

There, among the undead who moved in a confused manner, their prey disappearing into the ether, I recognized a familiar silhouette.

"Layla?"

I gasped. "Jamie?"

But the word was lost to the echoing silence.

CHAPTER ONE

LAYLA

SWEPT UP IN A RUSH OF WIND, I shot through time and space. I had no idea where I was going. All I knew was that my love, my Jamie, had spoken my name. Jamie. He wasn't dead. At least, he wasn't anymore.

I plummeted head over heels in a tunnel of light and darkness. Feeling like Alice tumbling down the rabbit hole, I fell slowly. Images of the undead flashed before my eyes.

The world is dead.

Jamie is dead.

No. Jamie is undead.

I hit the ground hard. Nearby, Kira and Susan whimpered. Frenchie spoke softly to them, comforting them.

"Where are we?" Kellimore asked.

"Safe," Tristan replied.

"Everyone all right?" Cricket asked.

There was muttered assent.

"Follow me," Tristan said.

Tristan led the others into the darkness. It was early evening. The heavy night had not yet fallen. The world around me glimmered with moonlight.

"You okay, Layla?" Will asked.

"Alive," I replied.

Kellimore reached down and helped me up.

"Where are we?" I asked.

Will shook his head.

All around us were walls of high green shrubbery. A strange mist swirled at our feet, and in the twinkling moonlight, the leaves on the bushes shimmered with blue light.

"Come on," Kellimore said, patting me on the back.

I turned to Will. "Did you see him too? Jamie? Did you see him before we went through?"

"Jamie?"

I nodded. "Just outside the cave."

Will shook his head. "No. Not since beyond the wall. Layla, I'm so—"

"No," I said, shaking my head. "No. He's not gone. I saw him. He was right there."

"Even if he was, he's not with us anymore," Will said carefully. "Layla—"

"I heard him. Here," I said, tapping my head. "He's not gone. He's like Elizabeth, the undead woman. I have to go back."

Will looked worried. "Are you sure?"

Kellimore looked carefully at me. "Come on, Layla. Let's catch up with the others."

The three of us followed behind Tristan and the others only to realize at once that the tall hedges were, in fact, walls.

"A maze. We're in a maze," I said.

We followed the sound of the others' voices as we navigated the twists and turns of the maze.

"This way," Tristan called once more. "Almost there," he added, and I could tell by the tone of his voice that he was trying to comfort Kira and Susan who were still whimpering softly.

Just as we reached the group, everyone stopped.

"What is it?" Cricket asked.

There was a brief paused then I heard Tristan say, "You don't need to wear that. The air isn't contaminated."

"I know," a soft, feminine voice replied. "It's just for the lime."

Frustrated, I maneuvered through everyone to the front of the group to join Tristan and Cricket. In the distance, I saw a massive old building, some sort of elaborate manor house. Candlelight glimmered from inside.

"Where are we?" I asked Tristan. I was in no mood for an adventure of his making. If Jamie was alive, or kind of alive, I needed to get back to Claddagh-Basel. I needed to know one way or the other. "I need to go back now. How can I get back? Jamie..."

Tristan shook his head. "First, we'll take shelter, decide what we can and should do," he said then turned to the young woman standing beside a wheelbarrow in front of us. She was holding a gasmask and looking at us like she'd just seen a ghost. No doubt our surprise appearance had set her on guard. She looked like she wasn't sure what to do—run or stand her ground. Her eyes moved over each of us slowly and carefully.

"You must be the ward. Is her majesty here?" Tristan asked the girl.

"Her majesty? What...who are you people? How did you get onto the property?" the young woman asked.

Just then, a black cat appeared from the darkness. Tristan's eyes went immediately to the cat, and then he inclined his head. "Your highness," he said.

Puzzled, I looked at the cat. The light around the animal changed, growing larger, brighter. Then there was a flash of blinding white light. A second later, an aged woman stood where the cat had been. The frail-looking lady coughed lightly then adjusted her gown.

"Tristan," she said.

She was one of the fae people. I cast a glance at the girl who looked both shocked and pleased all at once, as if the transformation of the cat had surprised her only a little.

"Where did the kitty go?" Susan whispered to Kira who shrugged.

I cast a glance back at my people. I had a duty to shelter them, and I'd made a promise to Frenchie that I'd always keep Susan and Kira safe. I would find out what happened to Jamie. Soon. I took a deep breath and stepped forward, moving around Tristan. "I'm Layla," I said, nodding to the old woman.

"I am Madame Knightly," she replied then turned to the girl beside her, "and this is Amelia."

The young girl, Amelia, smiled hesitantly at me. "Uh…" she started, seemingly unsure what to say. "Welcome," she said at last. "Welcome to Witch Wood."

CHAPTER TWO

LAYLA

WE FOLLOWED MADAME KNIGHTLY and Amelia toward the massive manor house.

"Your wards?" Madame Knightly asked Tristan.

"Here," Tristan answered.

The old woman linked her arm with Tristan's. "Then we have what we need."

"And Witch Wood? Are you secure here?"

"Yes," the old woman replied quietly. "As best as I can do."

Tristan nodded.

Amelia cast a glance toward me. Her eyes said so much, asked so many questions, but she didn't speak a word.

Madame Knightly led us through the front door of the grand estate. "Amelia," she said gently. "Please lead these people to the gentlemen's parlor, and let the others know they are here. And can you ask Logan to join me?"

"Of course," the girl said, leading us down the wood-paneled hallway of the massive old estate to an elegant sitting room adorned with fine Victorian-era furniture, books, polished tables, a billiard table, and glimmering brass décor.

"There are just five of us here," Amelia told us. "I think the others are in the dining room. I'll…I'll go get them," she said then looked us over. "Is anyone hurt?" she asked then, looking at Kellimore in particular, the bruises on his face still evident. I realized then that most of us were covered in some sort of blood or goo. "We have medicine, and I can help."

I glanced at the others. Chase was eyeing everything skeptically. He, Darius, and Ariel were staying close together. Vella's wide eyes also seemed on alert. Cricket was frowning at the door and, I imagined, at Tristan who'd left her behind. Elle, Tom, Frenchie and her girls, and Will just looked tired. This was it. This was all I had managed to save. Not only had I lost Jamie, but Ethel, Summer, Buddie, and Kiki were gone too.

"I shook my head. We'll be okay for now."

Amelia looked at Kellimore again. "You sure you don't have a headache or something?"

Vella shifted then looked at Amelia more closely.

"I'll be all right," Kellimore said, pulling on his tough guy mask.

She nodded then left.

I slumped down into a chair and put my head in my hands.

"Now what, Layla?" Will asked.

I shook my head. "Tristan will know. As for me, I need to go back to Claddagh-Basel."

"Why?" Cricket asked.

"Jamie."

"But, honey," she answered. "There is nothing you can do."

I shook my head. "Yes. Yes, I can." I looked at Vella. "I heard Jamie. I heard him as I have heard the others."

"Wait a minute, you mean the zombies?" Cricket asked.

"Not the rotted ones. There is nothing coming from them. But the others. You've seen it, right? The undead man who attacked the fox woman, I heard him too. And the woman, Elizabeth," I said to the Hamletville people who'd seen the undead woman Doctor Gustav had locked in the cage. "They aren't all gone. It's like some of them changed into something different."

"Ghouls," Vella offered.

"Jamie. I heard him. I need to get back. I need to try," I said.

"Those things, those fox people, are still going to be there," Elle said. "And the undead were everywhere."

"And don't forget the vampires," Chase added.

"Vampires," Will spat. "Yeah, well, we've about done them in."

"Either way, we've got no business going back until Tristan gives an all-clear." Cricket said.

Just then the door opened and a girl with long black hair entered. She was followed by a strikingly beautiful blonde woman who was maybe five years older than me.

"Ho-ly shit," the dark-haired girl said, looking around the room.

The blonde woman frowned at her then smiled at us. "Welcome," she said then. "Sorry, we're just surprised. We haven't seen anyone for months. Amelia said you came… through the maze?"

"We know," Vella answered. "It's strange to us too."

The blonde haired woman smiled softly at Vella. "I'm Beatrice. This is Zoey."

"Where are we?" Tom asked.

"Witch Wood Estate. In Brighton, Connecticut," Beatrice answered.

"Connecticut!" Tom exclaimed.

Beatrice and Zoey looked puzzled.

"This shit is so messed up," Darius said, sitting down.

"We were in Maryland…about an hour ago," Chase

explained.

Beatrice shook her head. "Well, I have no idea how you got here, but I bet these two little girls would love something to eat. We have dandelion soup, venison, and bread. Anyone hungry?"

"Dandelion soup?" Kira asked, looking puzzled.

"Like the flowers?" Susan added.

Beatrice nodded. "Please, come with me."

And with that, the blonde-haired woman waved for us to follow her. Beatrice led us to a massive formal dining room where Amelia was already setting out plates. The image of it startled me. I'd walked out of hell into a formal dinner party. At any moment I expected the Dormouse, March Hare, and Mad Hatter to show up.

Amelia looked up at us. "I know," she said then paused. "I know you are all…confused. It's going to be okay. Eat. Rest. You'll be safe here."

"How do you know that? Nowhere is safe," Kellimore said.

Amelia smiled as she set down the last tea cup. "Perhaps it's better not to waste time pondering riddles that have no answers."

CHAPTER THREE

AMELIA

AFTER GETTING EVERYONE SETTLED, I crept quietly into the kitchen where Madame Knightly, Logan, and the newcomer named Tristan were sitting at the breakfast nook and talking quietly.

"Everything all right, dear?" Madame Knightly called when she saw me.

I stared at her, playing back over in my mind how many times Bastet had followed me around. All that time it had been Madame Knightly. But how?

"I was just getting some towels and water. It's okay if they eat now, right? The little ones must be hungry."

Madame Knightly smiled kindly. "Of course, Amelia. And don't fret, dear. We'll have a good chat tonight. I know I have some explaining to do."

I cast a glance at Logan. He had a strange, guilty expression on his face. And I noticed the energy around him looked as confused. Over the winter, the relationship between us had grown stronger. Under Madame Knightly's watchful gaze, however, nothing had ever been taken beyond conversation and flirting, but my heart was brimming for him and his for me. There was no denying it. It was only a matter of time before the words were actually spoken.

But why had Madame Knightly asked for him? I mean,

after all, I'd spent the whole winter reading every book she set in front of me, from old folktales and Arthurian legends to books on herbal healing and wild-crafting. Madame Knightly was teaching me. So why hadn't she asked me to stay?

Turning away, I grabbed a jug of water, clean towels, and the basket of bread Madame Knightly had prepared. Just as I turned to go back to the dining room, Zoey entered the kitchen behind me.

"What's going on?" she whispered.

I shook my head. "No idea. So, I'm just going to serve dinner until I figure it out."

"They came through the maze? The maze? How the hell?"

"No clue. Want to help me grab the soup bowls?"

"They are all banged up. They said they just escaped a horde of zombies. I don't know. Something weird is happening. What's Logan doing?" she asked, looking over my shoulder.

"Madame Knightly wanted him," I replied then flicked my eyes toward the butler's pantry between the dining room and kitchen. Catching my drift, Zoey turned, and we headed into the pantry, the door to the kitchen swinging closed behind me. "Okay, so you know how the gates here are like—"

"Enchanted. So the maze must be some sort of gateway."

"But Zoe, that's not the big news."

"There's something bigger than living in an enchanted manor house with a magical maze?"

"Madame Knightly...have you ever seen Bastet and Madame Knightly in the same room?"

"Well, sure. I mean, sure. Right?"

"*Are* you sure?"

Zoey looked thoughtful. "Maybe...maybe not. What are you getting at?"

"She's been pulling a Clark Kent."

"What? No. No freaking way. No. That's not possible."

"Outside, when they showed up, Bastet was there. Then all this light surrounded her and *poof*, Madame Knightly was there, and Bastet was gone."

"So, you're telling me Madame Knightly is the cat."

"Yes."

"The cat."

"Yes."

"The cat is Madame Knightly?"

"Yes. That's what I'm saying."

"Then she isn't...human."

"I have no idea. But I know those people just appeared out of nowhere. And that man, Tristan, he has an accent just like Madame Knightly."

"And Logan," Zoey added.

"Logan?"

"You know, that accent you hear in his voice sometimes. The one he tries to hide."

She was right. I had noticed the accent, but I just thought it was an odd coincidence. But then again, the light around Logan was always a bit different, a swirl of indigo with other opalescent colors shimmering just around the edges. "Are you saying Logan is like Madame Knightly?"

"How the hell do I know? I mean, *I* wasn't the one who saw her turn from a cat into a woman. We'll ask them. Both of them. Later. In the meantime...I guess I better grab the soup bowls?" Zoey said, arching her eyebrows as she shrugged her shoulders in confused disbelief.

"Yeah," I said absently as my mind quickly patched everything together. What had Madame Knightly asked Tristan? Something about his wards? His wards. What did it all mean?

As Zoey pushed open the door to the dining room, she grinned then leaned toward me. "Suppose we have any more cat people in our midst? Should I grab the Meow Mix too?" she whispered.

"That's not even funny."

"You sure?"

"Well, maybe a little," I said with a wry grin then followed Zoey back into the dining room.

CHAPTER FOUR
LAYLA

I STARED AT THE ELABORATE TABLE setting in front of me. I could hear the others asking Beatrice and Zoey questions. Why had Tristan brought us here? What was I going to do now? What happened to Jamie? Even if he was changed, I couldn't just leave him there like that. I was just beginning to understand that not all the undead were so dead. Vella had called them ghouls. Maybe. Certainly, they were not quite human anymore. But they weren't quite dead either. Maybe all hope wasn't lost.

I looked around the room. Darius was whispering in Ariel's ear, trying to comfort her. Tom, Will, Elle, and Frenchie were keeping busy trying to entertain the girls. Chase nervously tapped his finely-polished fork against his plate while Amelia tried once more to give Kellimore something for a headache.

I gazed across the table to find Cricket staring at me, her forehead furrowed.

"Ya know what," she finally said, "when I was real little, my Grandma used to make me sit at the kids' table at Thanksgiving. We ate at the card table while the grownups sat around laughing and having a great time. I didn't like it then, and I don't like it now. How about you, Layla?"

I nodded. "Agreed."

With that, Vella, Cricket, and I rose and headed toward

the kitchen.

"Do you need something?" Amelia asked.

"Yes," I replied. "Answers."

My words silenced the room.

"I'm sure Madame Knightly—"

"We've seen enough, been through enough, to afford us a little impatience. Excuse us," I said to Amelia then turned back toward the kitchen.

The girl opened her mouth to speak once more, but her dark-haired friend set her hand on Amelia's shoulder and shook her head.

Vella, Cricket, and I passed the butler's pantry and entered the narrow kitchen. Tristan sat with Madame Knightly and a young man about Amelia's age. I cast a glance at Vella whose eyes narrowed as she looked him over.

"Cricket?" Tristan asked, standing.

"We decided we weren't keen on waiting around to see what y'all decided," Cricket told him.

Madame Knightly looked from Tristan to Cricket and raised an eyebrow, a slightly bemused expression on her face.

"Who are you?" I asked the young man.

"I'm Logan. Your name is Lay—"

"Are you fae too?" I asked.

Logan balked. He looked as if I'd slapped him in the face.

"They know," Tristan explained. "The unseelie revealed themselves to Layla and her people. And Layla knows Peryn. They know the truth about who we are and what the unseelie have done."

A guilt-ridden look crossed Logan's face. "Yes, I am. But Amelia and the others don't know about me."

Feeling annoyed, I turned back to Tristan. "I need to go back. I heard Jamie. He's not gone. I heard him. I need to go back."

Tristan nodded. "I was just telling Logan and Madame Knightly about some of the unusual things we've seen, how the unseelie's plan to wipe out mankind wasn't quite as effective as they hoped."

"It's the first I'm learning of the living dead, as it were," Madame Knightly said.

"We've stayed sheltered here in Witch Wood," Logan added.

"How?" Vella asked.

"I enchanted the grounds, pulled us a vibration or two out of sight from the human eye," Madame Knightly explained. "It's kept us out of view from the undead and the dark fiends."

"Then you know about the strigoi?" Vella asked.

"Oh my dear, they have always existed. And they will perish now that the world has died."

"And that fox woman? The kitsune or whatever? How many of her are creeping around?" Cricket asked.

"Many," Tristan replied then turned to me. "Layla, Witch Wood can be a new start. Madame Knightly has been training Amelia so she can—"

"So I can what?" a voice asked from behind me.

I turned to find Amelia standing there, a stack of bowls in her hand.

"So you can help keep everyone safe," Madame Knightly answered.

"That's all well and good for people here, but what about everyone else? What about other survivors, assuming there are any?" Cricket asked.

"Here, you are safe from the undead. But as long as the kitsune roam, mankind is in jeopardy," Madame Knightly said.

"Not to mention the strigoi," Vella added.

"Luckily, we've had no issues with them here," Madame Knightly assured her.

I felt relieved to know that the others, especially Kira and Susan, would be safe at Witch Wood—at least for the moment. But it wasn't enough.

"Tristan, I need to go back," I said then, looking from him to Madame Knightly. "And not just for Jamie. I know what happened to him. Doctor Gustav was experimenting. She infected him on purpose. But she never would have done that if she didn't truly believe she'd found a cure. The doctor may be dead, but her notes and everything else are still at Claddagh-Basel.""Claddagh-Basel College?" Amelia asked.

"Yes, that's where we were. I could go back to the lab and see if I can recover the doctor's work."

"Even if we find her notes, or the antidote, who among us will ever understand?" Vella asked.

"Beatrice," Logan said then looked at Madame Knightly with a surprised expression on his face.

Madame Knightly nodded.

"Will you take me back?" I asked Tristan.

"Yes, he will," Madame Knightly replied for him. "So, with that decided, let's eat, shall we?" she said then rose.

The ancient matriarch came forward and took my arm. "You've seen a lot. I know. Remember, we are here to help you. That is all we ever wanted. I will do everything I can. There is still good in mankind, as there always has been. The kitsune are blind to it, but we are not."

"How can we ever defeat them and survive all the rest?" I wondered aloud. Even if I could locate the cure, even if someone at Witch Wood could reproduce it, the world was still overrun with the undead, and vampires lurked in dark corners. All at once, it felt as if we really had no place left in the world.

"Well," Madame Knightly said kindly, patting my arm with her hand, "let's cross that bridge when we come to it."

"With all due respect," I replied. "The bridge is on fire, and we're standing in the middle of it."

"Then I guess we'd better figure it out quickly."

CHAPTER FIVE

AMELIA

"AMELIA, WAIT UP A MINUTE," Logan called as Madame Knightly led the others back into the dining room.

I turned and looked at him, once again seeing a shamefaced expression. I suddenly felt like I'd missed out on the best part of the conversation. As it was, my mind was still boggling over the idea that Madame Knightly and Bastet were one in the same. And what was the other thing they were talking about… strigoi? What the hell were strigoi? "Logan, what's going on?"

"I need to tell you something," he said. Taking the stack of bowls from my hands and setting them aside, he led me toward the front of the house and out the front door. It was very dark. The sky overhead was full of glimmering stars. The moon shimmered brightly.

Logan took a deep, shuddering breath. Gray energy swirled all around his normally indigo-colored aura. He was confused and scared.

I smiled gently at him then touched his face. "It's okay," I whispered. At once, the cloudy energy vanished.

"All right. Well…it was no accident that I came to Brighton. I was sent here," Logan explained.

"By whom?"

"My people."

"And who, exactly, are your people?"

"If I tell you, I'm not sure you'll believe me."

"Well, I just saw Bastet turn into Madame Knightly. Try me."

"Amelia...I'm not human. I'm fae."

"Sorry?"

"I am a son of the Tuatha de Dannu, the old people. I'm one of the seelie."

"The seelie?" I asked, my mind racing back to the legends of the old faerie people Madame Knightly had me reading about all winter.

"And so is Madame Knightly. And Tristan."

Well, that explained her reading selections. "But how? Why?" I said, not really even sure what questions to ask.

"My people foresaw mankind's end. I was sent to Brighton to keep watch on Miss Beatrice. The elders sent me, since I am, even among my own people, just a teenager. They asked me to attend the high school. They wanted me somewhere where I could be close to both Beatrice and you."

"And me? Why?"

"The elders saw that certain humans will be terribly important as the world crumbles. You. Beatrice. Some of the newcomers. The fae have been watching over you."

My heart was galloping. Logan had always felt special, but I'd just assumed it was because I'd pretty much fallen in love with him. Of course he was special. I never would have guessed there was so much more. "Why didn't you just tell me?"

"I couldn't. For one, I didn't have the words to explain it to you. Two, Madame Knightly told me not to. And we aren't supposed to get mixed up romantically with humans."

"Tristan and that girl with the blonde hair—"

"Cricket."

I nodded. "They seem to be—"

"Much to the elders' frustration. Amelia, you know I have feelings for you. With Madame Knightly here it wasn't possible to say more. Now, at least, I can explain. Madame Knightly is one of our chief elders. Even among the fae I'm still an apprentice. I had to do as she commanded."

The worried expression on Logan's face softened. I could tell he wasn't sure what to expect, if I'd be angry or sad. Goddess knows I'd never expected anything like this, but I didn't want to give Logan any pain. I cared about him too much. I smiled. "So, can you turn into a cat too?"

Logan laughed. "No. I tried to turn into a bear. Ended up with a nasty beard. It's not a skill I've mastered."

I chuckled. "Your aura…you were always different. I just didn't know why."

"And now you do. And I'm sorry. I wanted to tell you."

"I understand."

We stood there for a few minutes, gazing into one another's eyes. He'd never kissed me. Never confessed anything to me. But I knew his heart was mine. Gently, I took his hand then led him to the fountain. We sat along the edge.

"Layla said there might be a cure. Is she right? Do you really think there could be some sort of antidote, and that maybe not all the undead are lost?" I asked.

Logan nodded. "And there is more. Some of the undead seem to have transformed into a new kind of being. Layla has been able to communicate with them."

"Seriously?" I asked, thinking about my mother. Was there any hope for her? What if the cure actually worked? For all I knew, she was nothing more than a rotted corpse walking around my back yard. But still.

"I don't know. The elders never spoke of it. Our plan was only to find those humans to whom we were led and keep them safe."

"Well, so far so good," I said. "And now I know why Madame Knightly has had us cleaning all week."

"She must have known they were coming."

We both nodded.

Just then the door opened, and Zoey came outside.

"Any more shapeshifting cats out here?" she called.

I grinned wryly. "No. Just a faerie," I began then turned to Logan. "A faerie what? Are you a prince or something?"

Logan laughed and shook his head.

"Just some faerie dude pretending to be human," I told Zoey.

"Oh. Awesome," Zoey answered sarcastically.

"The girl with the curly dark hair said there are these things called strigoi lurking around. What are they?" I asked Logan.

He frowned. "You don't want to know."

"Try us," Zoey said.

"Strigoi is another word for vampires."

"Vampires?" I asked.

"Yeah, you were right, I didn't want to know," Zoey said.

Logan shifted uncomfortably. "The night walkers. They do exist, but in dwindling numbers."

"Well, that's a relief," Zoey replied. "So, you're fae?"

"Yes."

"Interesting. And we also have vampires. What about werewolves?" Zoey asked.

"Myth."

"Mermaids?" Zoey asked.

"Don't know. I don't swim."

"The kitsune? What are they?" I asked.

"Evil fae. They hate your kind and mine."

"Got it. So far, we've got vampires and really evil faeries

but not werewolves and maybe mermaids. How about swamp creatures?" Zoey asked. Linking an arm in mine and the other in Logan's. She led us back toward the mansion.

"Myth."

"Unicorns?"

"Alive once. Dead now."

"Well, that sucks."

"Yes."

"Dragons?"

"Same as unicorns."

"Damn. Cyclops?"

"All dead."

"Zoey?" Logan said then.

"Yes?"

"Shut up," he said with a laugh.

Zoey grinned. "Aliens?" she asked as we made our way back inside.

CHAPTER SIX

LAYLA

THE CHATTER IN THE DINING ROOM seemed strange and distant. I felt like I was having an out-of-body experience. Unmoored from myself, I stared down at my plate. How could I just sit there and eat when I felt like a piece of me was missing? I cast a glance at my engagement ring. Blood was smeared on the diamond. He was just gone. How had this happened? Jamie had died trying to find a way to save everyone, not just the Hamletville survivors but everyone. And me, I'd let the undead woman, Elizabeth, kill the only person who could have saved him.

Maybe, just maybe, if everything hadn't gone wrong, we would be working on producing a cure, undoing what the kitsune had done. Instead, Jamie had been turned into a... ghoul. Not dead. Not alive. Something different.

I pulled off the ring and slipped it into my pocket then cast a glance around the room. Everyone was eating, was trying to be okay. I couldn't fake feeling happy.

I rose quietly and exited the fancy dining room. The building was large and silent. I passed through a small parlor and down a long hallway until I found myself in an immense old library. I sat down and put my head in my hands and wept.

I had failed at the Harpwind. I had failed at Claddagh-Basel. I had failed to save Ian. I had failed to save Jamie. And I had failed Ethel and Summer and Kiki and Buddie and all the others from Hamletville.

I wept softly into my hands.

What was the use of trying anymore?

If I found Jamie, then what? What if he was gone or he tried to eat me alive? Or worse yet, what if he was whole inside his undead body? What was I going to do? I sat there and wept until I felt completely hollow. What was I going to do now?

"Big place," a voice said from behind me.

I turned to find Kellimore looking around the room.

"Not much for libraries. Spent more time on the football field, but I always loved history."

Shaking my head, and feeling miserable and stupid, I wiped away tears. "I…I worked at the Smithsonian."

"D.C., huh? I thought about Georgetown. The University of Alabama offered me the best scholarship, but I declined it. I wanted to stay in Ulster, go to Claddagh-Basel. My parents were pissed. I took a year off and coached at the high school. They were even more pissed. So, the Smithsonian, huh?"

"I was a curator, ancient weapons expert."

"Well, that's a good choice for a fencing coach," he said with a soft smile as he sat beside me.

"I need to thank you. You saved my life at Claddagh-Basel. I just…froze."

"Your boyfriend," he said then shook his head sadly. "I'm sorry. He seemed like a good guy."

"He is…was. I'm going back to Claddagh-Basel. I need to find Doctor Gustav's notes."

"That's what I heard," he said then rose. "Tell you what, I have a mammoth freaking headache and need some sleep. Tomorrow, let's get a plan going. In case those things are still there, or if the zombies, or vampires, or whatever else might be creeping around show up, we'll be ready."

"You don't have to go. I don't want anyone else to get hurt. Tristan said he would take me—"

Kellimore puffed air through his lips. "Tristan. Sure, he knew the college, but not the town. *I* know that town. Let me know when you're ready. I'll get you in and out of Ulster safely," he said then smiled gently at me. Though his words sounded prideful, his expression told a different tale. He wasn't bragging. He wanted to protect me.

"Kellimore...wait, that's your last name, right? What's your first name?

"Yeah....well, it's Kelly. Don't tell Elle. I don't want her to have something new to give me shit about," he said with a grin. "They are sending people upstairs to rest. Big house. Why don't you get some sleep? It's been a shitty day."

"Thank you, Kelly."

"Of course. Night, Layla."

"Goodnight," I replied then closed my eyes and leaned back into the leather chair.

Hold on, Jamie. I'm coming for you.

Just then, someone sighed heavily. I opened my eyes, thinking for a moment that Kellimore had returned, but was surprised to see my grandmother sitting in the chair where Kellimore had just been.

"Grandma?"

"I learned much from the dead. They used to tell me many things," she said. She rose and walked over to me then leaned in and brushed an otherworldly kiss on my forehead. The kiss was cold and incorporeal. "*But there are some things the dead cannot do,"* she said then disappeared.

CHAPTER SEVEN

CRICKET

"SO, YOU GONNA TELL ME HOW we traveled halfway across the country by stepping into a cave?" I asked Tristan as I slipped into bed beside him.

Tristan pulled me close, wrapping his arms around me, and kissed me on the shoulder. "Magic."

"Uh-huh. And just how does that magic work?"

"My people, our world, exists just beyond the perception of yours. It is a bit like bending space. There are magical places in your world, places where the old energy is strongest, where your world and ours touch closely. These places become doorways."

"And they are just all over the place?"

"Yes and no. They are usually found in natural places."

"So I couldn't just hop into a weird phone booth or something?"

Tristan chuckled. "No. That is a manmade thing. And besides, when was the last time anyone used a phone booth?"

"And this Madame Knightly? Who is she to you?"

"She is one of our elders. She's the mother of our queen."

"Your queen? Okay. And that boy?"

"He is just that. A young, but talented, man among our people. He was sent here to keep watch over someone."

"Over that girl? Amelia?"

"Madame Knightly had a special eye on her. He was keeping tabs on Beatrice."

"Why?"

"That isn't exactly clear. But, if she does have a mind for science…"

"Then maybe she could figure out what the doc was up to."

"Yes."

"Then you're going back."

"Yes, I will return with Layla."

"When do we leave?"

"We? *We* are not going anywhere. I want you here."

"Oh no. No more kids' table for me. If you're going to be my man…or faerie…or dog…or whatever you are…then you need to know we're equal in all things. I might love you, but my daddy always told me to never let a man tell me to mind my place."

Tristan chuckled.

"What? Don't laugh," I replied, feeling my fury stir in my chest.

"It's not that, my love," Tristan said. "You and Vella need to stay here. Vella will be able to guide us on the next steps, and she'll need you at her side."

I sighed heavily.

Tristan laughed. "I know my tilt girl isn't afraid of anything. But still. Stay here with Vella."

"You trying to protect me again?" I asked then rolled over and gazed into his honey-brown eyes.

"Protect you? Cricket, I would die for you."

"Now, don't get so dramatic," I said then smiled at him. "Your cat lady doesn't seem so crazy to see that you and I are knocking boots."

"It's not permitted, but as I explained to her, it cannot be helped."

"Why not?"

"Because I love you."

"Do you now?"

"You know I do."

"Then show me."

"How?"

I reached under the covers and slowly slipped my hands under his shirt, feeling his warm, soft flesh. "Oh, I can think of a few ways."

"Well," Tristan said as he drizzled kisses down my neck, "if that's what you have in mind, I'll probably be able to show you a few times tonight."

"I'll prepare myself to be educated."

Tristan laughed then pressed his lips against mine.

CHAPTER EIGHT

LAYLA

I WOKE IN THE MIDDLE OF THE NIGHT still sitting in the chair in the library, my grandmother's words fresh in my mind. The weight of them tied my stomach into knots. Groggy, I rose, grabbed my sword, and then headed toward the stairs. As I passed through the front parlor, I spotted Amelia asleep on a chaise. I stopped to cover her then went upstairs.

The second floor of the mansion was quiet. Only one door was open. I could hear Chase snoring inside. I followed the stairs to the third floor. The doors were closed, but Tom was sitting in the hallway.

"Layla?"

"Hey."

"Kellimore said you were in the library. We saved you that room down there," he said, pointing to a bedroom at the end of the hallway.

"Thanks. What are you doing out here?"

"Will and me…we thought we might keep watch tonight. Just in case. Frenchie and the girls are sleeping," he said, pointing to the door behind him.

"They okay?"

He nodded. "I checked a little bit ago. This place is quiet, seems safe. But it always *seems*. Learned that lesson real good."

"Yeah, haven't we?" I said. "I can keep watch for a bit. I'll get Will up when I'm too tired. Where is he?"

Tom pointed down the hall. "I asked them to keep all the Hamletville people together…what's left of us." Tom's eyes teared up. "I'm so sorry about Jamie. He was a good friend."

I nodded, fighting back my own tears.

"Did you really hear Jamie? Like you did with that zombie woman?"

"Yes. I…I think so."

"What does it mean?"

"I don't know. Maybe he's not lost. That's why I need to return."

Tom nodded. "I understand."

"Goodnight, Tom. Please, get some sleep."

He rose. "Goodnight, Layla."

Tom entered the room across the hall. Moving quietly, I cracked open the door to Frenchie's room. Inside, the orange glow of a candle lit the entire room. She and the girls slept together in a large bed in a luxurious room decorated in Victorian furniture and trappings. How peaceful they looked.

I closed the door gently then sat down, my back against the wall, and pulled my shashka out of its scabbard. Cutting a corner of my shirt off, I sat cleaning goo from the blade. Hopefully, somewhere in this old house, I could find a whetstone.

A door down the hallway opened and a very sleepy-looking Elle came out.

"Jesus," she said, jumping. "You scared me half to death."

"Sorry. Just keeping watch."

"Suppose the old lady would have a heart attack if I smoke inside the house?"

"Um, yeah. Definitely."

"You know what they say, don't piss off the faeries…that's

what she said they were at dinner. Faeries. Like legit faeries. This world is so fucked up, I don't know what to say. But I do know I need a cigarette."

I smiled at Elle. At the very least, she and Kellimore had survived Claddagh-Basel.

"You suppose if I go outside alone the boogeyman will get me?" Elle asked with a laugh.

"You want me to wake someone up to come with you?"

"Nah, I'll be all right," she said then headed down the hallway.

I started thinking about Claddagh-Basel once more. We'd need to return first thing in the morning, right after sunup. Maybe there was another way onto the property other than through the cave. If the kitsune were still there, that's where they would be waiting. But surely they wouldn't expect us to return. They would move on, look for us in other places. Could they find Witch Wood? Madame Knightly said she'd used some kind of magic to protect the place.

I slowly cleaned my blade. Not only were the kitsune out there, but so were the vampires. With Rumor gone and only her underlings left scouting for food, they would be easy to pick off. And not only that, I knew how to destroy them. The undead blood would end their lives. I needed to make sure I got samples, vials, something we could carry any time we left Witch Wood.

I sighed again and set down my sword. It was too much. It was too much for one person. I wrapped my arms around my knees and pulled them to my chest, resting my head on my arms. Too much. I tried to shut down my mind. I didn't want to think about it anymore. But every time I tried to clear my thoughts, Jamie reentered them once more.

"Layla?" he'd called.

"Layla?"

Jamie.

"Weird outside," a voice said, startling me from my dark thoughts. Elle had returned, smelling of the wind and tobacco smoke.

"Weird how?"

"Misty. There was a blue sheen to everything, blue lights sparkling everywhere. I felt like if I got a foot more away from the house the mist might have swallowed me up."

"The enchantment."

"Freaky."

"Worth it?"

"Totally. Now I can sleep," she said. "Night, Layla. Hey, make sure you get some rest. I mean, thanks for keeping watch, but I think we're safe here."

That's what they always say. "Goodnight."

After she closed the door, I looked down the hallway. There was a window at the end of the hall. She was right. The glowing rays of the moon and the glimmering stars were now occluded by heavy mist.

Safe.

Safe.

Where is safe anymore?

CHAPTER NINE

AMELIA

"AMELIA?" SOMEONE SAID AS THEY gently shook my shoulder.

I opened my eyes to find Madame Knightly peering down at me. "Good morning," I whispered.

"Why didn't you take one of the rooms upstairs? We turned on the heat."

I was lying on the chaise in the ladies' parlor where I'd spent the entire winter. I'd kept to my old spot close to Madame Knightly's room on the first floor in case she needed anything.

"Habit, I guess," I said, sitting up. "I wasn't sure if you might still need my help."

"Oh, Amelia," she said, sitting down on the chaise beside me. "It was never my intention to deceive you. I am an old woman either way around it, and I did need your help."

"I was always happy to do it." Madame Knightly had become as dear to me as a family member. Even after everything had gone bad, after Witch Wood had saved us, I'd gone on looking after her as I always had. Because the truth was, I loved her.

Madame Knightly took my hand in hers. "You're a good girl, a special girl. My people, they saw signs the end was coming. And it just happened that a very special girl lived in the town where I also happened to reside. I am old, and it's been a very long time since I concerned myself with things from either world—yours or mine. I've been living a quiet life here at Witch Wood. But Witch Wood is special. My people built this house, a place in your world, where my kind can be safe. There are several such places. My king asked me to sort out the signs, to discover what the kitsune were doing, and to keep my eye on that very special young girl."

"Tristan called you 'highness.' Why?"

"My daughter is now our queen."

"Were you once—"

Madame Knightly shook her head. "No. My daughter takes the role through her handfasting to her husband. I am a simple scholar. I saw the end was coming. The dark fae, once before they sought to kill mankind—"

"The Bubonic plague? I remember now...you were reading a book about it."

"Yes. They failed then. They succeeded this time."

"Layla said they aren't all dead. Something has happened to some of them," I said, relaying what Logan had told me.

"A complication no one expected. And something only a human, with her human magic, could see. My people are a little black and white at times. We chose to intervene and protect you, to save some of you. But what everyone has failed to see is that you are capable of saving yourselves."

"How?"

"Through the very thing that makes you human. The magic beneath your skin. The heart that beats inside you. The science of your minds."

"We are safe here though. Here at Witch Wood, the enchantment has—"

"Has prevented the kitsune and the night walkers from discovering you, has prevented the undead from finding this place. But it is a small place. Yet, there is still a chance for your people."

"The cure Layla spoke of."

"Yes. If they can recover it."

"If they can recover it. If it works. So many ifs," I said with a sigh.

"The world is always full of ifs. Now, let's go ahead and get our coats on."

"Why?"

"We're going outside, of course. It's time to start your training."

"What training?"

"It's time for you to learn how to find, and hide, Witch Wood," she said then extended her hand to me.

My body tingled from head to toe, the aura around me springing to life. After all these months, she was finally going to teach me.

CHAPTER TEN

LAYLA

THE NEXT MORNING, I SAT QUIETLY at the table as the others ate their breakfast. In the end, we were lucky. Hamletville had given my people shelter, Claddagh-Basel had protected Cricket's group, and Witch Wood had remained unscathed. But what about those who'd walked the hollow world without a home, without shelter, among the undead? I'd briefly seen what the human world had devolved into. How many innocent people had fallen to the grotesque brutalities of mankind? Were there other survivors still roaming the dead earth looking for food, water, warmth? And what of the undead who were…awakening…to their new form?

"Layla?" I heard someone call, and I realized then it wasn't the first time someone had said my name. I looked up to see Tristan looking at me.

"Sorry?"

"Claddagh-Basel. We were thinking it would be best to provision today, rest, then return tomorrow morning at sunup," Tristan said.

I looked around at the group. Tom, Will, and Frenchie were looking at me questioningly.

"We don't have to go back, do we, Mommy?" Kira asked.

"No," I told her with a smile, looking from Kira to Susan and then at the others. "I need to go back. I believe Doctor

Gustav developed a cure. I need to go back to the lab and try to find it," I said, casting a glance around the room.

"Beatrice," Logan said. "It might be helpful if you go with them."

"Me? Go out there?" A look of panic crossed her face. "But aren't they still out there? The zombies, and worse, from what you've been saying."

"They are," I said. "In and out. We'll come right back."

"How will you even get there?" she asked.

"The maze," Tristan replied.

"If we pop out at the cave, won't there be someone waiting? I mean, if they are smart, they left someone to keep watch," Chase said.

Tristan nodded. "There is another way into Ulster."

"Where?" Kellimore asked.

"Red Branch Grove. Do you remember a standing stone there, the one marked with Celtic knots?"

"Near the lodge? Yeah. I remember it."

Tristan nodded. "The stone was brought there many years ago. It is a doorway."

Kellimore nodded. "I know the place. And the best path to get you back to the college. I'll lead you."

"Thank you, Kellimore," Tristan said.

"I'll go," Chase offered. "You're going to need help if things get tight."

"No," Vella said. I noticed that she had her tarot cards lying in front of her.

"No?" Chase asked her.

She looked up at him, her dark eyes speaking volumes. "No. You will stay."

The room went silent.

"Kellimore, Logan, Beatrice, Layla, and I will go," Tristan

said.

"Me too," Will added.

"Please," I said, looking at Will. "No. Please stay here. I need you here."

"Layla, you sure?" Will asked.

I nodded. "Please stay," I replied, shooting a glance at the girls.

Frenchie smiled softly at me.

"All right," Will replied, understanding.

"Are you sure you need me?" Beatrice asked.

Tristan nodded. "We won't know what to look for without you."

She took a deep breath like she was steeling her nerves.

"We need to get ready. You got ammo here?" Kellimore asked Logan.

"No."

"Great," Kellimore said with a frustrated huff.

"But there is a whetstone in the storage shed," Logan told me.

"Well, that helps. But we need something else," I added then. "Have any syringes?"

"Like medical syringes?" Zoey asked.

I nodded.

Zoey looked at Beatrice who shook her head. "No, I don't think so. Why?"

"We should have them ready, just in case."

"The zombie blood?" Will asked.

I nodded.

"Zombie blood? What for?" Zoey asked.

"Apparently it is lethal to vampires."

"Maybe I can write down what to look for," Beatrice said then with a shaking voice. "I…I don't know if I can do it.

Vampires?"

"We'll be back before dark. This is just a precaution," I told her. "In case things don't go as planned."

"When has that ever happened?" Will muttered under his breath.

"We need to go into town," Logan said, turning to Zoey. "Where can we go to get ammo and syringes?"

"I have an idea for the ammo," Zoey offered, "assuming no one else figured it out already. Syringes? We'll ask Amelia."

"Where is Amelia, anyway?" Beatrice asked then.

"Outside," Logan answered.

"Doing what?" Zoey asked.

"Learning to keep us safe," Logan said with a smile.

CHAPTER ELEVEN

AMELIA

"CAN YOU SEE THE GATE?" MADAME KNIGHTLY asked as we stood on the driveway just outside of Witch Wood.

"One second," I said, then looked hard, trying to see past the enchantment. I knew it was there. Today, however, it was nearly impossible to see.

"Still trying to see it with your eyes?" Madame Knightly asked me tartly then chuckled. "Try to see what only you can see, my dear."

"I can sense it," I said, lifting my left hand. "I can feel it, the energy brushing against mine."

"Yes," Madame Knightly said. "That's right."

The gate felt different. Before, its vibration had just felt off. Now, it felt deeper, further away. "I keep trying to feel it, but I just can't break past the illusion hiding it."

"That's because there is no illusion hiding it," Madame Knightly said.

I lowered my hand and turned and looked at her. "What do you mean?"

"Can you sense Witch Wood? Is it still there?"

"Yes."

Madame Knightly nodded then joined me, threading her arm through mine. "Do you remember the story of King Arthur and the Isle of Apples?"

I tilted my head. "The story of Avalon?"

She nodded slowly.

"When King Arthur died, Morgana moved the island, sank it into the mists, away from the human realm, to protect Arthur and the mysteries of Avalon."

Madame Knightly nodded. "There is no enchantment here, my dear. To the human eye, Witch Wood no longer exists."

"But I feel it."

"Yes, you do. *You* do. But Witch Wood isn't here."

"Then *where* is it?"

"Oh, just left a bit," Madame Knightly said, laughing lightly, "for lack of a better way to explain it. I moved it."

"To where?"

"The otherworld."

"Your world? The world of the fae?"

"No, not into our world either, just...in the middle."

"How? How did you do it?"

Madame Knightly nodded. "That's what you must learn, to see the shadow world and live in it. It is old magic." Madame Knightly smiled and patted my hand. "Now, the trick is," she said, pointing where the gate should be, "knowing that it's not hidden. No matter how hard you look, you will not see the gate because it's not in this world. You must loosen yourself, let the magic inside you feel the otherworld. It's like having a hard shiver, and there you are. You must see. See what others cannot, and trust your mind's eye in all things, Amelia. Your mind's eye sees the world just beyond this one. And everything in that world is real, just as real as the light you have seen around others all your life."

"Even if I can see, how can I lead others through the space?"

"All you have to do is believe. The others don't need to see. They just need to believe in you. Now. Let's go back. Go ahead," she said, motioning to the misty abyss where the gate should have been.

"Are you asking me to believe in you?" I asked then, smiling wryly at Madame Knightly.

"Oh, my clever girl. Of course I am, but," she said then paused, nodding toward the gate, "but in this moment, it is *you* who must believe. You must believe in yourself, in what you have known all along."

"That there is more to our world, more just outside common vision," I said, staring at the space where the gate should be.

"Yes."

"That there are more worlds, more magic in this life, than the human eye can see."

"Yes."

"And that I was born seeing it," I said with a whisper. And then, I was suddenly struck with an odd feeling. A tremor moved down my body, shaking me from head to toe. And in that moment, I felt the air around me shift and clear. All the energy, the auras around everything became vivid. It was like the world was alive with light. I could see Witch Wood, its energy, its…life. And the moment I saw that, the mists fell. Once more, Madame Knightly and I were standing before the gate. Behind us was a thick mist, the veil between the real world and this strange space. My skin rose in goosebumps.

Madame Knightly clasped her hands together. "Well done."

I smiled.

"I suppose the others will be getting ready to go out. You must go with them."

"Of course."

"Very good," she said then pushed open the gate.

I passed behind her then paused to close the gate behind us.

"Tomorrow, we'll practice again," Madame Knightly said. And with a blink of blinding light, she shifted once more into the form of Bastet. Meowing once at me, she turned and trotted back toward the house.

I shook my head.

This was going to take some getting used to.

CHAPTER TWELVE

LAYLA

I STEPPED OUTSIDE INTO the crisp morning air. Inside the shed, I found gardening and farming equipment, including modern tractors and old hand-held plows. There was enough equipment in the barn to run a small village. And from the looks of things, that's how the residents had been living. The greenhouse was full of seedlings, and the fields nearby had already been tilled.

Leaving the door open to let the light and air in, I scanned for the supplies, finally finding oil for my blade. I sat down at the old whetstone, large and suitable for grinding axes, and began working on my shashka.

How many nights did I sit in my Georgetown apartment, staring out the window and caring for my blade? It was my link to the past. It was the only thing I'd taken with me from Hamletville except my memories and the ink on my arm. It was a skill that, in the end, had kept me alive. But just me. Not Grandma. Not Ian. Not Jamie. Just me. Where was the justice in that?

When I was done, I slid the blade back into the scabbard and rose. I felt cold in my long-sleeved shirt. Spring had come again. I shook my head. If we had just stayed in Hamletville, everything would have turned out so differently.

"Layla? You ready?" Logan called.

Logan, Amelia, Zoey, Chase, and Darius crossed the lawn toward me.

I smiled when I saw Chase. "Vella let you go this time?"

"Yeah, she said Brighton would be okay. Took a little convincing though. We wanted to make sure you had enough muscle. Kellimore and Tom rounded up all the guns. We've got a list of what we need."

"Thank you," I said with a smile then turned to Darius. "You slipped out too?"

"Can't let my 'cuz have all the fun," he said, grinning at Chase.

"Zoey said you need syringes," Amelia said carefully. "There should be some at my house. My stepdad was diabetic."

I nodded. "Okay. I'm ready."

"Hour walk," Zoey said. "We'll try to grab a car in town."

"Slow and easy," Logan added. "We don't know what state we'll find Brighton in. The undead will be around, and we don't want any of the kitsune to discover us."

"Awesome," Zoey said, and then I saw her pull a handgun from the back of her jeans. "Three shots left."

At this point, I had no idea where my guns had gone.

"I'm packing," Chase said, turning to Amelia. "How about you?"

"Oh, don't worry about her," Zoey replied, shooting Amelia a glance, but she didn't elaborate.

Chase, Darius, and I exchanged looks. Just what we needed, another wild card.

We headed down the driveway to the old gate enclosing Witch Wood. Amelia opened the gate, and we stepped outside into the foggy morning air. It must have been almost noon. I was surprised to see how the mist lingered. But then I noticed it was only lingering outside the gate, not inside.

"You've got it?" Logan asked Amelia quietly.

"I think so," she whispered.

When I turned back to see what they were talking about, I was confused.

The gate was gone. The estate was gone.

Logan and Amelia were standing in front of…nothing. The girl was concentrating hard, Logan watching her. I heard her whisper something just under her breath then silver light shimmered where the gate had been, and a chilly breeze swept through.

"Okay," Amelia said, exhaling deeply. "Okay, I think I've got it."

"Are you seeing what I'm seeing?" Chase whispered to Darius.

"If you're not seeing anything, then we are seeing the same thing," Darius replied.

"Layla?" Chase asked.

I squinted hard. I could feel the place, I just couldn't quite see it. "I…I'm not sure."

"All right, then," Chase said, shaking his head.

"It's…good, right?" Zoey asked. "Can you—"

"I can get us back in," Amelia answered.

"Let's go," Logan said, and we headed down the road.

"How did you do that?" Chase asked Amelia. "The whole place. The walls, the building, they're just gone."

"It's *like* an enchantment," she explained.

"It's how we've stayed safe all this time," Logan said.

"What about you guys? Where were you all this time?" she asked, turning to Chase and Darius.

"We found our way to Claddagh-Basel College with Tristan's help. We were there almost since the beginning. Found Elle and Kellimore there."

"What about you, Layla?" Zoey asked.

"We were in our hometown. We had things locked down, but we were tricked. Some people offered us shelter at an island in the Great Lakes. We went. It was a trap. They brought us there…as food."

"The night walkers," Logan said.

"Yes. My people killed their queen. Some came to Claddagh-Basel. Jamie and I figured out how to change them back into their human form. The blood, such as it is, of the undead restores them back to their natural state, their natural age, which destroys them."

"Jamie…he was your boyfriend?" Amelia asked gently.

"Yes," I replied quietly, mindful of the ring in my pocket. It had just felt too strange to continue to wear it. The hope the ring stood for was now shattered.

* * *

Brighton sat in a little valley between rolling mountains. Zoey led us down a back road at the edge of town. Tall weeds grew out of cracks in the pavement. We kept quiet. Soon we found a vantage point slightly above the town that gave us a good scope of the streets. There we could see a few undead wandering aimlessly. They were in a heavy state of decay.

"You remember my dad's friend, Moonshine Pete?" Zoey asked Amelia.

"The guy who used to ride a bike around town with a cooler strapped to the front?"

"That's the one. He had lots of guns."

"If he's still alive, the chances of us getting shot are relatively high," Amelia said.

"Yeah, there is that. But he knew me, for better or worse.

Always liked to squeeze my ass when my dad wasn't looking. His place is down on Second. We can stop there, drop by the Feed and Supply shop, see if there is anything left, then head to your place."

Amelia nodded.

"You know to aim for the head, right?" Chase said to Zoey.

"Yeah, figured that out the hard way," she told him with a wink. "Ready?"

We nodded.

Zoey led the way. As we wove silently down a side street, I couldn't help but notice how the town looked untouched. It was like the world had just stopped. Cars still sat in driveways. Bikes were ditched in yards. When the virus came, it must have swept over the town quickly. If that was the case, chances were good that many of the residents were still inside their homes and probably not alive anymore. In Hamletville, our system of clearing out the houses had worked well and kept the town safe. The people of Ulster had done much the same. But Brighton was different. The world had died overnight here.

Motioning for us to stop, Zoey peered around the side of a building then came back.

"Well, we've got a problem," she reported.

"What?" Chase whispered.

Zoey put her finger on her lips and motioned for us to listen.

When we did, we could hear the groans of the undead. From the sounds of it, there were a lot of them.

I moved slowly around Zoey and peered out. We were across the street from a two-story house with faded white paint. The house was completely surrounded by chain-link fence. Inside the fence, someone had created a system of elaborate holding pens. Inside those pens were the undead. My eyes quickly scanned the place. Whoever Moonshine Pete was, he'd created a fortress to protect himself. Heaps of undead corpses laid piled just outside the front door. The undead inside the pens were heavily decayed. The gate blocking off the walkway was closed.

"I think it's secure. The undead are locked up," I said then stepped out.

"Oh my Goddess," Amelia whispered when she saw the sight.

"Must be twenty or more," Zoey said.

"How are we going to get through?" Darius asked.

"We don't. Can't risk it," Logan said.

"If you need to go back to Claddagh-Basel, you need to be ready. You sure he's got guns?" Chase asked.

Zoey nodded.

"Let's have a look," I said then made my way toward the property. A rusted chain kept the gate closed. With a heave, I dropped my blade on the chain. It felt to the ground with a clunk.

"Oh," Amelia said, covering her nose.

"Now, that's a smell," Zoey added.

"Breathe through your mouth," Chase told them.

I scanned the undead. "*Anyone? Is there anyone here?*" I called with my mind. There was no one, nothing but a bunch of rotted corpses. The undead pressed their pulpy, decaying faces against the chain linked fence. Flesh melted off them.

"When you get the syringes, we can come back here. They're all penned up," Darius said.

"Actually, that won't be necessary," I said, and with a quick wave of my sword, chopped off one of their hands. I picked it up by the finger, looked it over, and then dropped it again.

"Maybe not. Too dry."

"I might be sick," Zoey said.

Logan shook his head. "We never saw anything after the first days."

"Be ready to haul ass, and don't get bit," Darius told him.

I suddenly wished we'd brought more muscle. I knew Chase and Darius had my back, but the others were ripe to the hell the world had become.

We moved toward the porch when Amelia suddenly reached out and stopped me. "Wait," she said. She scanned the house.

"Amelia?" Logan asked.

"Something is…off," she said

"Pete," Zoey called. "Pete? You in there?"

My eyes spotted movement in the house. In an upstairs window, an undead man pressed himself against the glass. His mouth was open wide.

"There," Amelia said, pointing.

"Well, there's Pete," Zoey said.

"Should we expect anyone else at home?" Darius asked.

"No. He didn't have anyone."

Moving past the heap of corpses, we made our way to the front door.

"Well, looks like we won't be going in this way," Zoey said, pulling a piece of paper off the door.

"To whom it may concern. If you can read this, I'm dead. One of those assholes bit me today. The first floor is wired with explosives. If you want what I got, better start climbing. And when you're up here, please shoot my sorry ass," Zoey read.

"Well, that was thoughtful," Chase said.

Zoey shoved her gun in the back of her jeans again. "All right, Pete," she said, grabbing the rail of the porch and heaved herself up. Grabbing for a handhold, she grasped the edge of the roof and pulled herself over, throwing her body onto the roof of the porch.

I saw Chase raise his eyebrows in appreciation then pass Darius a knowing glance. Darius nodded.

"The roof is rotted. Come slow," she told us.

"Why don't you and Amelia stay here," I said to Logan. "It will be easier to drop the guns down to someone, assuming we find them."

"All right," Logan said. "Okay, Amelia?"

"Yeah," she said absently, staring out at the undead caged up in the pens.

With that, I followed Zoey.

"Here," Chase said, boosting me.

I moved slowly across the roof toward a hallway window. Chase and Darius followed carefully behind.

"He's loose in there, but we shouldn't shoot if we don't have to," I said.

Zoey nodded.

"Cricket lent me this. For close encounters," Chase said then, unsheathing the machete he had strung to his belt.

"Let's go," I said.

I turned my face as Darius smashed out the window pane with the butt of his rifle.

The noise echoed across the silent valley.

"Better keep an eye out for company now," I said, noticing that the undead below were even more riled up.

From inside, we heard a ruckus as Moonshine Pete shambled toward us, practically throwing himself out the window.

"Back," I motioned to the others, and the second he poked his head out, I swung.

His severed head rolled off the roof, smashing onto the concrete sidewalk like someone had dropped a watermelon, brains and goo splashing everywhere.

"Sorry, Pete," Zoey called.

"Well, he won't be grabbing anyone's ass again," Chase said.

Zoey smirked.

Pushing the rest of Pete's corpse out of the way with my boot, I went inside. The house smelled putrid. The scent of decay, locked up behind closed windows, was horrid. Coupled with what must have been fecal remains and rotted food, I had to swallow hard.

"Remember, breathe through your mouth," Chase reminded Zoey who suddenly looked a bit green.

"This way," she said then, waving us toward the room where we'd first seen Pete. Inside, we found exactly what we were looking for.

"All right now," Chase said.

On a long table, Pete had been making shotgun shells. Guns lined almost every wall, including several automatics. And once again, I found grenades. They were more modern than those Grandma had procured, but they were grenades nonetheless.

Zoey grabbed a tote bag.

"We'll take it all," Chase said.

"I can't believe they're all still here," Zoey said as she packed the bag. "Makes sense though. It all happened so fast. It was like it just swallowed us, like a wave of death," she said with a shake of the head.

Darius tossed a bag to me. Moving quickly, I started shoving ammo inside. Through the window, I saw even more undead coming toward the house. They had heard the window pane break. Through the window, however, I saw Logan run to the end of the walkway and close the gate, wrapping the lock with the broken chain.

"Shit," Chase said. "We can't get pinned down here."

"Layla? Zoey?" Amelia called.

"Let's go," I said, stuffing three grenades into my coat pocket. We headed back out onto the roof and handed the bags to Logan and Amelia then climbed down.

"We need to find another way out," Logan said, eyeing the undead blocking the path.

I shook my head. "No. We've got this," I said, motioning to Chase.

Moving to the end of the walkway, I stabbed the few undead who'd gathered then opened the gate. Chase followed me, and we quickly finished off the undead who were closest to us.

"They're going to have to get their hands bloody," Chase said then, looking back at the others.

"They'll learn."

"Clear, but we need to move," I called.

"Well, let's hope they learn fast," Chase said and we headed back out into the dead world.

CHAPTER THIRTEEN

AMELIA

I TRIED TO HIDE HOW MUCH I was shaking at the sight of so much…death. We had seen the moment the world ended but nothing after. The whole world had gone dim. The light around everything had faded. It was all so dark, so black, as if all the life had been sucked out of the world. As much as I thought I was ready for it, I wasn't. Not even a little.

"Are you all right?" Logan asked.

I shook my head. "It's all gone. All the colors. It's just gone."

"No. You are alive. We all are. There is still life," Logan said.

I didn't respond. I didn't know what Logan could or couldn't see, but what I could see was that the world was nothing more than a husk.

Moving quietly, we worked our way down Ash Street toward the old feed store. Brighton was just rural enough that the local feed and tackle store stayed in business. We were hoping it hadn't already been looted.

As we moved, Layla, Chase, and Darius worked together, cutting down the zombies that crossed our path. Their hands, unlike ours, seemed practiced. For Chase and Darius, it was a job that had to be done. For Layla, however, something about her energy changed every time she swung her sword. The sword itself had a glow, a dark blue hue. When she wielded it, the aura around the girl and the sword melded and became one, both glowing brightly. The sword was an extension of her, and she an extension of it. I could see from her face that she didn't love the killing, that wasn't what was making her sparkle. It was her love of the blade, the craft of using it. It was the same glow all people took on when they practiced something they were really good at, something they were born to do. I used to see that same aura around Mom. How many times had I seen her moving quickly down the hallway at the hospital, rushing from one patient to the next, the soft pastel colors around her glowing like her spirit might burst from the shell that confined it?

I was heading home for the first time in all these months. What condition was I going to find her in? Would she still be there? Would she be a rotten and decayed corpse like the zombies roaming the streets of Brighton?

Zoey whistled to the others then pointed toward the shop. Out front were several trucks. Bodies lay on the ground in various states of decay. Inside one of the trucks, an undead man struggled to get out.

"Mister Johnson," Zoey said, looking him over. "Used to come into Studio. Likes his coffee black. Was always flirting with Janice."

"You want me to…" Chase offered, motioning to the knife.

Zoey shook her head. "He's good where he is," she said then leaned into the back of his truck and pulled out an axe.

"Company," Layla called. Spinning her sword like a baton, she readied herself as six undead men came lumbering out of the feed store.

"Stay back," Logan whispered, stepping in front of me.

With the others distracted, I closed my eyes and pressed my hands together, feeling the energy pulsing around them. The old ways. The old magick. All winter, Madame Knightly had been giving me things to read. Humans had once been close to the Earth, close to our Great Goddess. As a Wiccan, I knew this. As an aura reader and healer, I understood that magic was real. But it wasn't until my encounter with Larry that I knew how real. That was the first time my white light had manifested in the material plane for something other than healing. It had been an accident. But slowly, I was learning that I could wield my power.

I opened my eyes to see Layla and the others making short work of the zombies. Then I heard a terrible gurgling sound behind me. I heard the groan, and then the terrible smell of death wafted toward me.

I turned to see a zombie woman lumbering our way. Her jaw hung slack. She must have just eaten…something. Blood dripped from her chin. What had she eaten? An animal? A person? I almost called out to Zoey, but then I thought better of it.

"Stay here," Logan said to me and moved forward to help Zoey. He didn't see the undead shuffling our way.

I turned and stared down the zombie woman, studying the darkness around her. Flickering light, soft tones of blue, fought against clouds of black. Like a flame struggling to come to light and burning out over and over again, the blackness surrounded her, eating up the light.

I took a deep breath, looked down at my hands, and envisioned a massive ball of swirling white light therein.

Now or never, Amelia.

"Amelia," I heard Layla call as the zombie woman came near, too near, to turn back.

"No," I yelled and with every bit of energy I could muster, I sent the white light spinning forward. I could see it in my mind's eye, blasting toward the zombie woman.

The undead woman's body rocked when the light hit her, and she stumbled backward. I watched the white light snake around her, infecting the darkness. She reeled then stumbled toward me again.

"Amelia," Logan called, rushing back toward me.

Calling up my energy again, I envisioned a fiery ball of light. I sent the light flying from my hands.

This time, when it struck her, the undead woman fell to the ground.

"Amelia?" Logan said. "Amelia, are you okay?"

Chase, Darius, Zoey, and Layla joined me. Chase and Darius were looking at me with confused expressions on their faces. Layla regarded me closely, her green eyes assessing.

"Told you she'd be fine," Zoey told Chase as she shook blood off the axe.

I looked at the others. "I...I'm a witch," I told them.

Chase laughed, shaking his head. He wiped the blood off his blade then shoved it back into the sheath. He then looked at Darius. "I'm beginning to think we're the only people to survive the apocalypse who aren't psychic or something."

Darius laughed. "Well, at least we're in good company."

"What about you?" Chase asked Zoey. "Secretly a werewolf or anything?"

"Do I look like a werewolf?"

"Girl, when you have some time, I'd love to run down how I think you look," Chase replied.

Red flashed in Zoey's cheeks. That was a first.

"Shut up," she said, but she was smiling at him. "You okay, Amelia?" she asked me.

Shaping my hand into a finger gun, I blew off the illusory smoke.

Zoey laughed.

"Let's go see what we can find," Layla said, motioning to the building. Before she went in, she turned and smiled at me, her eyes meeting mine. Her energy shifted, softened, and I could see from her expression that she understood. She nodded gently then turned and went inside.

"I'll try the trucks," Darius said. "This town is full of zombies. We're going to need a ride."

I followed behind the others, Logan alongside me. "Your training is going well," he whispered.

"But I don't want to hurt anyone or anything," I said, looking back at the undead woman lying on the ground. The dark light all around her was gone, as was the blue light that had struggled to survive. Now she was very still, very silent. There was no glow to her. There was nothing.

"They're already gone," Logan said. "Don't let it trouble you."

"Are they?" I asked, thinking once more about the fighting glimmer of blue light.

I walked into the store and grabbed a bag off the wall as Layla and Chase cut down the last two zombies still inside.

The place smelled nauseating. The cooler, which had once displayed local cheeses, was completely overgrown with green mold. In the freezer beside it, cuts of meat sat in the same state of rot. The shelves, which had once held canned goods, were all empty.

"Someone has been here," Zoey said, tapping her nails on the shelf.

"Who?" I mused.

Zoey shrugged.

"We've got wheat and corn here," Layla called from the back.

"Propane tanks. Small ones," Chase said.

From outside, we heard a vehicle door open followed by a grunt. A moment later, we heard an engine sputter, reluctant to start. After a minute, however, the engine clicked on.

"Too much noise," Layla said. "We need to be fast." Sliding her sword back into her scabbard, she picked up a bag of grain, carrying it on her shoulder.

Nodding, Logan and I lifted a bag of corn and went outside.

"We can plant a whole field with this. Feed a lot of people at Witch Wood," Logan said with a smile.

I nodded, but I was overcome with feelings of regret. How many people in Brighton had died because we hadn't offered them shelter at Witch Wood? It hadn't been my choice, I knew that, but the guilt nagged at me. Hiding at Witch Wood wasn't the answer, but I didn't know what was. The idea of a cure, however, was something I could trust in. But how do you cure a walking corpse, their eyes bulging out of their heads, their limbs missing? There is no cure for that.

Moving quickly, we headed outside. As it turned out, it was Mister Johnson's truck that started, his corpse now lying on the ground, his head bashed to bits. We loaded the truck with supplies as Layla and Chase kept watch. So far, it was a good haul. Guns, ammo, and now some food. Just one last stop.

The hardest one of all.

CHAPTER FOURTEEN

LAYLA

AMELIA SAT IN THE FRONT WITH DARIUS directing him toward her home. We could see signs of small arms fire all around town. There were many dead bodies littering the streets, and someone had tried to barricade the small library only to have failed as evidenced by the bodies lying all over the sidewalk on both sides.

"They didn't stand a chance," Chase said.

I shook my head. "Overrun just like that."

I thought back to the first days in Hamletville. They'd been hard, but we'd stayed together. We'd worked as a team. Kellimore and the others had saved Claddagh-Basel. Here, no one had made it.

The truck pulled into the driveway of a small house and parked beside a green Volkswagen Beetle.

Amelia exited the truck then went to an enormous oak tree that sat at the side of the driveway and lay her hand on the trunk, her eyes closed. After a moment, she turned to us. "I'll go in and grab the supplies. Be back in just a minute," she told us.

"We'll go with you," Logan said, motioning to Zoey.

The expression on Amelia's face saddened me. She looked as if she were about to burst into tears. Was it just the loss of everything or something more? I frowned, an odd feeling nagging at me. Something more was going on here.

"What do you think?" Chase whispered to Darius.

"She's hot," Darius said. "Lots of attitude. Good fit for you."

Chase laughed. "Zoey? Oh yeah. But I was talking about Amelia. Did you see what happened? She pulled an X-Men move back there. What the hell was that?"

"New world order," Darius said with a shrug. "After all the times Vella has saved us with her cards, I guess I just roll with it now. You shouldn't be worried about mutant powers. Instead, better keep your eye on shorty with the attitude. What do you think, Layla? Good match?" Darius asked.

"Leave me out of it," I said with a grin, but then I looked at Chase. "But yeah. I'd work on that if I were you," I said then lowered the tailgate and sat down.

Chase chuckled, and then he and Darius started strategizing about Zoey. I rolled my eyes and pulled out my shashka. I was about to start cleaning the blade when I felt a soft brush against my mind. It was almost like I heard someone take a sharp inhale.

"Daughter. Daughter. Home."

"Oh shit," I said then jumped off the back of the truck and raced toward the house.

"Layla?" Chase called.

I rushed quickly inside, scanning all around, looking for the source of the voice, trying to hear.

"Hello? Hello? Where are you?" I called, my eyes searching.

"My daughter. Amelia."

Amelia, Logan, and Zoey were in the back of the house talking in low tones. I could hear drawers opening and closing. From the tone in her voice, I could tell Zoey was trying to comfort Amelia.

Now, I knew why.

"Where are you?" I called to the unseen voice.

There was a pause, as if the undead had not expected to hear anyone.

"Here," the voice replied, and a moment later, I saw a shadow on the curtains hanging in front of the sliding glass doors. *"Here."*

Darius and Chase entered the house behind me.

"Layla? Everything okay?" Chase asked in a low voice.

I nodded, motioning for him to be silent.

Moving slowly, I drew back the drapes to find a woman standing there. She was wearing faded and stained medical scrubs, her feet bare, her hair a matted mess. But she wasn't decayed. She wasn't in the same rotted state as the others. She was one of them.

"Can you hear me?" she asked, her cloudy eyes searching my face.

"Yes."

"Who are you?"

"Layla."

"Where is Amelia?"

"No," Amelia yelled from behind me. "No, Layla. Don't," she said, rushing across the room and grabbing my arm.

Logan and Zoey hurried into the room behind us.

Amelia had gone absolutely pale, the color draining from her cheeks.

"Mom," she whispered, a tear trailing down her cheek.

"Look away, Amelia," Logan said. "Layla, close the curtains."

"No," the undead woman said.

"Your mother?" I whispered to Amelia who nodded sadly.

"Mom," she said softly. She gently set her hand on the glass.

The undead woman groaned oddly then she set her hand on the window opposite her daughter.

Amelia gasped. "Mom?"

"I…I can hear her," I whispered to Amelia.

The girl's brow furrowed. She stared at me. "How? But she's gone," she said, but then I saw her look more closely at the woman, squinting to see something we could not. After a moment, she gasped.

The undead woman dropped her hand and turned away.

"Mom?"

"The hunger. I must fight it."

"What's happening?" Zoey asked.

"Mom," Amelia said then, "her energy is still inside her. I see her colors. I can still see her in there. The darkness is all around her, but her colors, I still see them."

"What's your name?" I asked the woman.

"Can't. Too hard. The hunger."

"Your name? Please."

"I was…Caroline."

"Caroline," I said then.

Amelia gasped then grabbed me. "The cure! We need to get that cure."

I nodded. "I left my fiancé behind. He was like her, undead but not gone. Nothing will stop me. We will find the cure."

"Mom," Amelia said then, setting her hands on the glass. "Mom, can you hear me? These people might have a cure. Mom! Mom? Mom, can you hear me? Mom, I love you!" she said then wept.

Logan wrapped his arms around her, Amelia practically crumpling into a heap.

"Amelia. Love you."

"Amelia…she says she loves you too."

CHAPTER FIFTEEN

CRICKET

"LET ME SEE IF I'VE GOT THIS RIGHT. Madame Knightly can keep this place hidden so we could just ride things out here and see if Beatrice can figure out the doc's notes?"

"Yes and no," Tristan replied.

"Oh good, yes and no, just what I wanted to hear," I replied, frowning at Tristan across the small table in the breakfast nook in the kitchen.

Vella, busy shuffling her cards, completely ignored us.

"Cricket," Tristan said carefully. "The magic will deceive the undead and the vampires, but the kitsune will be able to get past the enchantments eventually, as they did at Claddagh-Basel."

"At Claddagh-Basel? There were spells there?"

"Yes, very old ones that protected the place. But they were not strong enough. I was not strong enough," he said, looking defeated.

Great, now I'd made him feel bad.

"You did what you could," Vella said. "The undead were only the beginning. This is a bigger fight."

I raised an eyebrow at Vella.

"Okay, okay. Maybe so, but what I'm talking about is truly surviving in the long run. We need to figure out how to make that happen," I said.

"You must defeat the kitsune," Tristan said.

"And how are we going to do that?"

Tristan frowned. "You cannot. We, my people, must end it. As long as you live, they will seek to extract vengeance."

"Can you think of no other way?" a soft voice called from the other end of the kitchen.

We all stopped and looked back to find Madame Knightly standing there.

"Your highness, I didn't hear you come in," Tristan said.

"Oh, slipping around on all fours this morning," she said then poured herself a cup of tea. "I get around faster like that. Now," she said, joining us at the table, "what do your cards say, Vella? What is the path?"

Vella shook her head. "There is war here, but that is not all."

"What else do you see?" Tristan asked.

"*The Hermit*."

"And what does that mean?" I asked her.

"We must withdraw."

Tristan sighed heavily.

Madame Knightly smiled. "Patience, Tristan. Peryn's ward will not cease her quest, and we must let her try."

"Peryn's ward? You mean Layla?" I asked.

"Yes," the old woman said with a soft smile as she sipped her tea. "Ah, now that's nice."

"You think there is a chance for the cure?" I asked, looking from Madame Knightly to Tristan. "'Cause I don't know about you, but the undead I've seen creeping around don't look like they'd survive even with a cure, not now."

"As Layla said, they aren't all the same," Vella added. "If she can hear them, then they are not gone. There is a chance."

"Perhaps, perhaps not," Madame Knightly said. "But if

there is one thing that is certain about mankind, you always fight to survive, until your dying breath. And, perhaps, beyond. We shall see."

I frowned at the woman. I had just about had my fill of all this mystical crap. If the doc had found a cure, and we'd just left it behind, then we had to go get it. Every single one of us could still turn into one of those things.

"When are you going back to Claddagh-Basel?" Vella asked.

"Tomorrow at sunrise."

Vella pulled a card and set it on the table.

I looked at the card. It was "*The Fool*" in the upside down position.

She shook her head. "It won't come easy."

Tristan nodded. "Nothing ever does."

"I'm going with you," I told him.

"See what I mean," Tristan said, grinning at me. "Not this time, my lovely tilt girl."

"What, you gonna try to make me stay home?" I asked him with a grin.

"No, but *I* will," Vella said.

"Man alive, you two are so irritating," I said with a groan.

Madame Knightly laughed. "Come on, Cricket. I'll make you a cup of tea," she said then smiled. "It always calms my nerves."

"Better put a shot of bourbon in it."

Madame Knightly held her teacup to my nose.

The scent of alcohol wafted from the dainty porcelain cup.

"Why do you think it's so effective? Some problems call for more than chamomile."

At that, we all laughed.

CHAPTER SIXTEEN

LAYLA

THE OLD TRUCK ROLLED DOWN the quiet streets of Brighton, stopping once more at Moonshine Pete's where Chase and I filled a dozen syringes with the blood, such as it was, of the undead.

Amelia sat in the back of the truck staring off in the distance. She hadn't said a word since we'd left her house. I didn't blame her. Her mother's voice had come across so loudly, so clearly. It was the same with Elizabeth, with the man in Ulster, with Jamie, and with my Grandma. Grandma had told me to kill her, to shoot her. And I had done as I was told. But now I questioned myself. If I had heard her, did that mean she was like these others? Not decaying zombies, but something else, still carrying a flicker of life inside. I sighed.

"That's odd," Zoey said.

"What?" Chase asked.

"There," she said, pointing. "You see? The courthouse. Top floor. You see that flicker of light?"

In an upper window of a large brick building at the center of town there was a shimmer of light. It was there for just a moment then it was gone.

"Maybe something sitting in the window?" Chase said.

Zoey shook her head. "I don't know. It's gone now."

After we'd filled the syringes, we left again. With Logan

guiding Darius, the truck turned down some bumpy back roads then finally onto the old dirt road that led to Witch Wood.

"How did you end up out here?" I asked Amelia, wanting to draw her attention away from her dark thoughts.

"Oh," she said, wiping a tear from her cheek. "I've worked as Madame Knightly's caretaker for the last few years. What about you? Where were you *before* all this mess started?"

"I was in D.C. I worked for the Smithsonian. I was a museum curator, taught fencing classes for middle and high school students."

"Sounds like a great life," Amelia said.

"It was," I replied. But was it? At the time I had thought so. Saturday morning scones at the café, teaching fencing three nights a week, hours in the dusty stacks at the museum. It had felt so great. But I was also terribly lonely. I'd worked hard just so I could ignore it. But it was always there. It wasn't until I'd returned to Hamletville that the feeling of loneliness had finally gone away.

"What about you? Where are you from?" Zoey asked Chase.

"Me and Darius lived in a little nowhere place in West Virginia. We're cousins. Darius was studying to be a teacher. I was studying because my mama told me I had to," he said, laughing. "I wanted to own a garage, be a mechanic. I'm pretty good with cars, actually. Anyway, we got flushed out of town, traveled with the Army when everything first fell apart," he said then shook his head. "Things went bad. We were on the run for a while. Took shelter in a run-down shopping complex for a bit. That's where we met Ariel. Then we ran into Cricket and Vella. Got cleared out of that place too. It was people that time. Bad people."

"How did you end up at Claddagh-Basel?" Zoey asked.

"Tristan took us there. We spent the winter there. We had some skirmishes with the undead but it was quiet, and we survived."

"We lost a lot of people at the college," I told them. "Good people." The image of Summer and Ethel falling to the undead flashed through my mind, paining my heart.

Amelia took my hand. The minute she did so, I felt the heaviness that had settled over me lighten. "I'm sorry. Your fiancé, and the others, I'm so sorry."

"Thank you," I said, squeezing her hand. I closed my eyes and tried to block out the tears. When I did, the image of Ian standing over me, holding my shashka, crossed my mind. "Too much death," I whispered.

"Yes," Amelia said.

"Then let's start focusing on living," Chase said, patting me on the shoulder. "They're gonna need you frosty tomorrow, Wonder Woman."

"Wonder Woman? That's a new one," I said with a smile. I squeezed Amelia's hand then let go. "I could use an invisible jet."

"How about an invisible house," Darius called from the front as he pulled the truck into Witch Wood's driveway.

Amelia climbed out of the back and walked over to the front gate. She stared at the place where the fence line should have been.

Logan joined her. They spoke in low tones then Logan stepped back.

I looked around at the others. Everyone was watching Amelia except Zoey, who was peering down the road in the direction we'd just come.

"Something wrong?" I asked.

She shook her head. "No, not really. I don't know. I

thought I saw something. Animal, maybe. Don't know."

"Animal?" I asked, immediately feeling alarmed. "*Did* you see something?"

"No, I mean, I was just guessing. I didn't see anything specifically."

"Well, if you ever see a fox, it usually means we're screwed," I said then stared down the road with her.

"Why?"

"The bad fae, the kitsune, that's the form they shift into."

"Great," Zoey said. "I don't know. It was just the wind I guess."

A moment later, I felt a chill fall over me. My skin rose to goosebumps.

"Well, look at that," Chase said then, causing both Zoey and me to turn around.

When we did, we found ourselves standing outside the gate at Witch Wood, the bright daylight shining down. And the road and forest around us? Nothing but mist.

I looked at Chase.

He shook his head.

Amelia looked back at Logan and smiled. She turned and opened the gate. Darius drove the truck through, and Amelia closed the gate behind us.

Amelia slid into the front seat with Logan and Darius, and we drove to the front door of the house. Tristan, Cricket, and Will came outside to meet us. In the distance, I saw Susan and Kira chasing bubbles across the lawn. They were wearing angel wings and rings of spring flowers on their heads. Madame Knightly stood beside Frenchie, laughing as she watched the girls.

"How did it go? Everyone okay?" Tristan asked, looking us all over.

"All good, captain," Logan replied with a wink.

"And we're stocked up now," Chase said, showing Tristan the haul of weapons that we'd brought.

"And I have the syringes," I said, patting the bag where I'd stashed them in.

Tristan nodded. "Then let's get some rest. Tomorrow at dawn, we'll head back through the maze."

"Thank you, Tristan," I said.

Tristan put his arm around my shoulders as we headed back toward the house. "If it were Cricket, there wouldn't be a thing in this world that could stop me either. And if we can work out Doctor Gustav's cure, it's worth a try. Layla, I never had the chance to tell you how sorry I am. I knew Doctor Gustav was obsessed, and I sensed her drive could prove dangerous, but I never thought she'd go so low."

"She tried to give it to Kellimore too."

"You're certain she is dead? There's no chance she survived the onslaught?"

"No. She's gone. We saw it. She was keeping an undead woman locked up in the college, experimenting on her. The lab got overrun, and the woman killed her." I didn't want to go into any further details, because the truth was, *I* had killed her. In my anger and frustration over what she'd done to Elizabeth and the baby, I had set Elizabeth free and stepped aside while she destroyed Doctor Gustav, and had felt righteous in doing so.

And I had paid dearly for it.

"Then I guess we are on our own," Tristan said.

Because of me…

CHAPTER SEVENTEEN

LAYLA

THE NIGHT PASSED QUIETLY. Tom, Will, and Frenchie stayed close to one another. They seemed relieved. For the first time since we left Hamletville, it felt safe at Witch Wood. We were, after all, being watched over by three fae guardians in a house surrounded by magic. We could live here quietly, without risking anything. In time, the vampires would die out and the undead would rot to the ground. But they weren't the only problems. The kitsune wanted us gone. Though I was leading the charge, I knew that going back to Claddagh-Basel was a mistake. We would expose ourselves. I knew it, but there was nothing that could have stopped me. I needed to know what happened to Jamie.

At dinner that night, I picked at my meal of rice, snap peas, and canned peaches.

"Not hungry?" Kellimore asked as he took a seat beside me, his blue eyes searching my face.

I turned to answer him when I realized he looked different. "Your hair!"

He laughed and ran his hand over his freshly shaved head. "Elle helped."

I looked at her. Elle was grinning at Kellimore. I noticed she'd re-shaved the undercut on her own hair.

"Used a straight razor," she said with a wicked grin. "I told

Kellimore he was brave, considering what a dick he's been in the past."

Madame Knightly, who was sitting at the end of the table, cleared her throat, passing Elle a look.

"Sorry," Elle said sheepishly.

"Yeah," Kellimore assented. "You're right, but that's all in the past. I had some growing up to do. Thanks for the shave. Now I'm aerodynamic," he said, sliding his hand across his head.

"I like it," I told him.

"I hear that if you rub a bald man's head three times and make a wish, it will come true," Elle told me. "Kellimore wouldn't let me try."

I had to laugh. I set my hand on his head. "Smooth," I said with a grin.

Kellimore chuckled.

I smiled to myself then looked up to find Amelia looking from Kellimore to me. A soft expression crossed her face. She turned back to her meal.

"So, sword sharp for tomorrow?" Kellimore asked me.

"Yeah, I'm good to go," I said with a nod, shifting uncomfortably. Amelia's glance made me feel awkward. I turned back to my food. "You ready?"

"Loaded like we're headed to the Wild West."

"We might be."

"You think so?" Beatrice asked then. "That it might be bad?"

"Nah, they're just kidding, I'm sure," Elle answered for us. "Either way, I convinced Tristan to let me come too. I mean, I know the place. It will make it easier."

I nodded, glad to hear the news. Elle was no slouch, and if we got pinned, she was handy to have around.

"We'll be careful," I told Beatrice who looked very unsure.

I cast a glance at Madame Knightly who had just given Tristan a knowing—and warning—look.

I slid out of my chair.

"Thank you, Madame Knightly," I told her.

She nodded kindly and the others wished me well. In my room, I pulled off my boots and pants and crawled into the magnificent four-poster bed which was covered with a lovely crocheted coverlet. The gauzy curtains on the windows glowed in the moonlight.

I closed my eyes and tried to think about Jamie.

"I'm coming," I whispered. "I'm coming for you."

But as I drifted off to sleep, Kellimore's smiling face came to mind. Too tired to thwart it, I fell asleep thinking about his lovely topaz-colored eyes.

CHAPTER EIGHTEEN

LAYLA

I WOKE UP EARLY THE NEXT MORNING. To my surprise, I found a pile of neatly folded clothing sitting on the table just inside the door. Crossing the room, I lifted the bundle to investigate. There were heavy, tan-colored pants, a clean white T-shirt, and a long-sleeved flannel shirt. Hidden underneath, someone had left me clean underwear and socks. In that moment, such items felt like a godsend.

I looked down at the shirt I was wearing. I hadn't realized it, but the collar was stained with old blood, the hem ripped where I had cut the fabric to clean my sword and in a vain attempt to help Buddie. I was a mess. I stripped off my old clothes down to my undershirt and panties then grabbed the bundle. I paused to look outside. It was still early. The sunrise cast shades of pastel pink and gold across the horizon. Outside, I saw Chase and Kellimore returning from the shed, both of them carrying shotguns.

Their voices rose to my window. Chase was giving Kellimore a hard time about something. Kellimore laughed. How old was he? Maybe twenty by now. Five or so years younger than me.

I smiled at them.

Kellimore must have noticed movement in the window because he looked up, catching sight of me. He moved to wave but then quickly looked away, fighting back the smile creeping across his face.

I gasped and stepped back. Well, at least I wasn't completely naked. Caught gawking at him in my underwear though. I felt stupid. And just why was I doing that anyway? I shook my head.

"Okay, Layla. Focus."

There was a washbasin on the dresser and fresh water in a pitcher beside it. I stared at myself in the mirror. Dirt was smeared across my cheek, and my hair was a disaster. Sighing, I lifted a cloth and washed my face and body. The small bar of soap smelled like roses. The scent took me back to the night of my senior prom.

I was sitting in front of the mirror in my room at the cabin on Fox Hollow Road when my grandmother came in.

"My Layla, Ian just pulled up. How beautiful you are," she said as she smoothed my long, dark hair, gazing at me in the mirror. "Why do you look so sad?"

I sighed. "Ian and I had an argument last night. We're always fighting. I just want tonight to go well."

My grandmother sighed then sat down on the bed. "Your mother always had to have a man. From the time she was a little girl, she wanted to get married. So, she chased every man she saw. She chased, and chased, and chased something none of them could ever give her."

"What?"

"Love for herself. Your mother never learned to love who she was. I tried very hard to teach her, but she didn't listen to me or the spirits or anything else. She always looked for a man to love her. Layla, you don't need to have a man to be enough. But if you want a man, then find a good man. If he sees your value, he will prove himself worthy. Then you will know he's a good man. But make him prove himself first."

"Like Grandpa Sasha did with you?"

My grandmother laughed. "Yes. But I also saw my own value. Sasha needed to work to get me because I was worth it. I was a beautiful Russian girl who could see the otherworld. Of course the man who wanted me should work for me. Don't chase those who are not worthy of you."

"There is good in Ian."

"Perhaps, but he's not ready to show it yet. Layla, if a man loves you, he will be there for you, be gentle, and come to you slowly, with care and respect. Wait for a man like that."

"You're describing the perfect guy…who doesn't exist."

"I'm only describing what you deserve. Because you, my Layla, are special," she said then kissed me on the forehead.

I sighed then closed my eyes. There had been good in Ian, I was right, but he waited until the last moment to let it show. After Ian, after I moved away from Hamletville, I had tried to live by my grandmother's words. I knew she was right. But still, I saw that I had some of my mother in me. There were many times I had to rein myself in before I went chasing the wrong kind of guy. My relationship with Jamie, however, had simply snapped together. That was why I couldn't give up on him now.

I lifted the old brush off the bureau and pulled it through my dark hair. I stared at myself in the mirror. I looked thinner, worn. There were dark rings under my eyes. How lush my former life had been with its organic smoothies, veggie burgers, and endless hours on the treadmill. It all seemed meaningless. Setting down the brush, I dug into the bureau. There, among a number of intricate vintage hair combs, I found a rubber band. I pulled my long black hair back into a braid then rose and got dressed. I attached my shashka bandolier style across my back, slid my doe and wolf poyasni back into my boots, then picked up a handgun I'd grabbed in town. I checked the ammo. I was fully loaded. I shoved it into the back of my pants.

Sliding my vest on, I headed toward the door. Before I exited, however, a strange chill swept the room. I looked back to see my grandmother standing at the window.

"Grandma?"

She clicked her tongue at me. "My Layla," she said, pointing toward the dresser. "Don't forget the grenades," she added then disappeared.

I grabbed the three grenades sitting on the dresser beside the water gun filled with holy water. Shaking my head, I stuck the grenades and the water gun into my vest pocket. I glanced back at the window and frowned.

Definitely not a good sign.

* * *

Outside, Tristan, Logan, Elle, Kellimore, and Beatrice were getting ready. Madame Knightly and Amelia were standing nearby. Beatrice looked decidedly nervous. She smiled at me, her eyes drifting to the sword.

"I used to teach too," I told her. "Fencing," I said, pointing to the sword.

She smiled. "I went to Columbia," she told me then. "I studied microbiology. I loved teaching, but it hadn't been my first plan. I had a scholarship to get my MD. I just…my mother got sick."

"I'm sorry."

She nodded.

"Bring them back in one piece, then?" Madame Knightly said to Tristan and Logan.

Logan, who was still a bit of a puzzle to me, bowed politely to Madame Knightly then passed Amelia a knowing look.

Tristan nodded but his eyes were scanning Witch Wood. I followed his gaze to see Cricket looking out at him from a window.

She waved to him. I could see from the expression on her face that letting him go wasn't something she wanted. I wondered why none of her people had come. The worry settled in on me even greater when I saw Vella standing in the shadows just behind Cricket. What had Vella seen?

"Let's go," Tristan said.

We turned and followed him into the maze.

"Back into the lion's den," Elle said. "We're either stupid or crazy."

"Or both," Kellimore agreed.

"Let's try to have a positive attitude," Logan said lightly.

"Easy for you to say. Can't you just shift into a bird or something?" Elle asked.

Beatrice looked sidelong at Logan.

"No, I cannot."

"Does that mean you're special, Tristan? I hear you can shift into a dog," Elle said jokingly.

Tristan laughed. "Not special, just older than Logan."

"Ah," Elle said with a smirk. "Well, you know what they say about old dogs and new tricks..."

"Elle?" Tristan asked.

"Yes?"

"Shut up," he said playfully.

She winked at him.

We wound through the hedge maze until we reached the very center where there was a gazebo and reflecting pool.

"We're here," Tristan said, looking into the water.

"That's not where we came out," Kellimore observed.

"No. Different doorway to a different exit."

"You'll need to show us. To teach us," I told Tristan. "We need to learn these passages as well."

Logan cast a glance at Tristan.

"What?" I asked.

"I'm not permitted. You should discuss it with Peryn," Tristan replied.

I frowned.

"Who's Peryn?" Kellimore asked.

"Our leader," Tristan said. "Let's go. Take a deep breath and hold on," he said then stepped into the pool. The light therein shimmered blue, the water bubbling heavily at the surface. Tristan disappeared and didn't come back.

"Come on," I said, taking Beatrice by the arm. "It's just like riding a rollercoaster." Before she could protest, I led us both into the water. We both gasped for air as the water sucked us under.

I held onto Beatrice's hand as we were pulled downward with terrible velocity. I felt heavy pressure on my chest. My lungs screamed for air. I cast a glance at Beatrice who spun beside me through the dark space. Her eyes were wide. A moment later, I was grabbed from below and pulled with such great force that it ripped our hands apart. Light and sound passed all around me, roaring with terrible thunder.

"Peryn," I whispered in my mind. *"Peryn?"*

My body jerked sideways, and I was dropped into a sunny meadow. I rose carefully, not recognizing the place. The sun shone brightly. Everything felt too yellow, too bright. The flowers in the field were red, fire orange, and rich gold. In the center of the field, Peryn stood watching me.

"Layla?"

"Peryn, what should I do now?"

She smiled softly at me, but it grew harder and harder to see her as the sun glimmered onto my face. I covered my eyes, but the sunlight became brighter and brighter.

"Survive," she replied.

Suddenly I felt myself falling backward, tumbling through the air, and sucked back into the vortex.

A moment later, I landed hard on the ground.

CHAPTER NINTEEN

LAYLA

I OPENED MY EYES SLOWLY.

"Are you all right?" I heard Logan ask.

"Yes," Beatrice breathed. "I'm okay."

"Up you go," Kellimore said, offering me an arm.

"I'm never going to get used to that," I grumbled, standing. I dusted the dirt and leaves off my clothes. "Thanks."

His eyes lingered on my face a long moment. "Any time," he replied with a smile then turned toward the others.

Shaking off the feeling Kellimore's gaze had stirred up in the pit of my stomach, I pulled my sword and looked around. If the kitsune knew about this doorway, they might have someone watching. We were in the middle of the woods. There was a tall standing stone nearby. On it was carved a Celtic triskelion. Nearby was a large log cabin and a dilapidated archery range.

"What is this place?" Elle asked.

"Campground," Kellimore said. "The Sons of Red Branch and some church groups used it. Now, the only problem is that we are on the opposite side of the lake from the college."

"Can we make it there and back by nightfall?" Logan asked.

Kellimore considered. "Assuming there are no complications, yes."

Tristan nodded. "The cave is probably compromised but

close if we get in a bind."

"Either way," I said. "We're here. Let's go."

"This way," Kellimore said. "There are hiking trails all around the ridge of the valley. We can get about halfway there before we intersect with the first road. After that we'll be in town. For now, we're in the woods."

"And the woods have ears," Tristan said. "Let's go quiet. Kellimore, take the lead. I'll follow. Layla, you got the rear?"

"On it," I replied, and we headed out.

"Jamie?" I whispered with my mind. *"Jamie, where are you?"*

There was no reply.

We walked under the shimmering sparkle of new green leaves. The woods smelled sweet. There was no whisper of decay. New ferns uncurled their fingers and purple violets grew on the forest floor. This is what the kitsune were trying to protect, an Earth that looked like this. In that regard, mankind was a blight. We needed to change our ways, that was certain, but exterminating us had not been the answer. In the end, it was their last resort. And it had been effective—for the most part.

We walked for at least an hour before we started to see houses not too far from the path.

Kellimore motioned for us to stop. "The trail ends ahead. We'll follow Red Branch Way until we get to Blarney Drive. It will lead us to the college. We'll have to go in the front gate."

"The gate was compromised. It's open," I said, remembering how Buddie had done everything he could to defend us, protect us, and how it had cost him his life.

"We'll also be very exposed," Tristan added.

"How many undead were here?" Logan asked.

"A lot," Elle said.

"They may be gone now, wandered off," I added.

"Maybe, maybe not," Kellimore replied.

Beatrice shifted nervously.

I grinned at Kellimore. "Remember what Logan said? I was trying to be positive."

"And here I took you for a realist," he replied with a grin.

Logan smirked.

"When we get in, we'll go straight to the lab," Tristan said.

"The kitsune unbarred the doors on that end of the building. They'll be open. It was…a battle in there," I said then, hoping to prepare Beatrice.

Understanding, she nodded.

Kellimore motioned for us to follow him. We exited the woods at Red Branch Way. I remembered then that the town was arranged like a sun cross. I glanced up at the street signs as we walked. I needed to remember the way back just in case… in case Kellimore didn't make it.

No. I wasn't going to lose anyone else.

Not again.

We moved quickly. The quaint and quiet houses of Ulster were just as still as they had been the week before. In fact, it was too still.

"Too quiet," Elle said, echoing my thoughts.

I nodded. "I don't like it."

"Maybe the zombies followed those fox people out of town," Elle said.

"I hope."

We wove down a side street then up the steep incline toward the college. As we got closer to Claddagh-Basel, the scent of the undead became stronger.

Kellimore stopped.

We huddled.

"Smell it?" he whispered.

We nodded.

"We shouldn't go directly to the gate. Anywhere nearby where we can get a look inside?" I asked.

"This way," Kellimore said then led us across a series of lawns to a big house that sat not too far from the wall surrounding the college.

The scent of death grew even stronger, and from the other side of the wall, we could hear the groans of the undead.

Kellimore led us through the fenced back yard of a ranch-style house. Behind the house was an enormous oak tree, a treehouse perched on the upper branches.

"Franklin's house. Used to play with Emmie and Lucas here. Their family moved away. The treehouse never came down. You can see onto the college grounds from there."

"May be rotted. Be careful," I told him.

"Of course," he said with a grin then climbed up, grasping the old wooden steps nailed into the tree.

We watched in anticipation as Kellimore climbed. Elle scanned the perimeter, her gun drawn. I noticed she was also wearing a huge hunting knife on her belt. When Kellimore reached the tree house, he reached out and undid the hatch door.

A moment later, we heard a strange grunt and watched a body fall from the treehouse to the ground. The undead who'd been hiding inside the treehouse—no doubt still living when he went inside—hit the ground with a thud, his head smashing open, brains and goo splattering all over our feet. The smell was horrendous.

Beatrice suppressed a yelp.

"Great," Elle whispered, kicking bits of head and brain off her feet.

Waving his rifle into the space first, making sure it was

clear, Kellimore slipped into the treehouse. He poked his head out the window and panned around, looking through a pair of binoculars. After a few minutes, he climbed back down.

Shaking his head, he crossed the lawn.

"Not good," he said.

"How bad is it?" Tristan asked.

"The undead didn't leave. They're all still there," he said.

"Jamie? Jamie, can you hear me? James? I'm here!"

Nothing.

"We could try to sneak in along the wall," Elle suggested.

"No," Tristan said.

"Diversion," I offered. "We need something to lure them out. I do have grenades."

Kellimore grinned. "Of course you do."

Tristan shook his head. "Too much noise. It may attract the kitsune. We need something more subtle."

"Well," Elle said thoughtfully, "I suppose these kitsune might not think much of a random stray dog. Quiet. Uneventful. But it would be enough to lure the undead out of the way," she said, looking at Tristan.

"You suggesting I go in as bait?" he asked, raising an eyebrow at her.

"Um, maybe?"

I looked from Elle to Tristan.

"It's a good idea," Tristan said. "Even though I think you just suggested it so you could see me shift."

"I resent that remark," Elle said with a grin.

"How many are there?" Tristan asked Kellimore.

"They were all over. Maybe five dozen, if not more."

"I'll get them out," Tristan said then looked at Logan. "If something happens to me, you'll have to take them back through."

Logan nodded.

"You got this?" Tristan asked, turning to me.

"Yes."

Tristan looked at Kellimore. "I'll pull them out and then west. Stay here until it's clear, then head directly to the lab. You, Layla, and Elle can pick off any strays. Hand to hand."

"Not all strays, of course," Elle said with a wink.

Tristan rolled his eyes and with a nod to Logan, he turned and strode down the fence line toward the gate. Suddenly, a glow emanated from him. I winced and looked away. When I looked back, a mottled-colored mutt was running where Tristan had been.

"Well, now I've seen everything," Elle said.

"Can you head back up?" I asked Kellimore, looking toward the treehouse. "We'll hide around back until you give the all-clear."

He nodded. "Just don't leave me up there. I don't want to end up like him," he said, looking at the dead body on the ground.

I motioned for the others to follow me around the back of the house. Kellimore took his position in the treehouse once more.

The forest behind the house was silent. I could hear the call of a dove roosting nearby. My heart was beating hard. I closed my eyes and said a silent prayer that Tristan stayed safe.

A few moments later, we heard it. The groan of the undead rose up from the other side of the wall.

I heard a low, muffled bark, followed by more groans.

And then, we waited.

And waited.

Not risking a look around the corner for fear of being seen, I kept my eyes on Kellimore's silhouette as he surveyed the grounds. It felt like it took forever when finally Kellimore signaled to us.

Moving slowly, my sword drawn, I came out from hiding, the others following behind me. The smell of the decaying undead was horrid.

"Jamie? Jamie?"

There was nothing.

"Let's go," I whispered. Kellimore joined us, and we started moving slowly down the fence line toward the gate.

The scene inside was horrendous. Dead bodies littered the once-manicured campus grounds. Moving carefully, we stepped over the broken gate, trying to make as little noise as possible.

Kellimore motioned to the others, and we cautiously walked toward the medical wing of the college.

After we passed over the gate, I slowed. His body was unrecognizable except for the shredded shirt that clung to his bones. But the bow and quiver lying on the ground beside him was all the evidence I needed that the mangled corpse had once been Buddie.

I reached down and grabbed his bow and quiver. I fought back my tears, remembering the day in Hamletville when Buddie had appeared out of nowhere, saving us when the undead crashed the barricade.

"Buddie, I'm so sorry," I whispered, feeling swells of grief and anger. "The kitsune will pay." No one else was going to die because of them.

"Layla?" Kellimore called softly.

Holding my sword tightly, slinging the bow and quiver on my back, I rejoined the others.

As we neared the building, Kellimore signaled for us to slow. The door to the medical wing of the college was open.

From inside, we heard muffled groans.

"They could be anywhere," Elle said.

"We'll go into the lab and close it behind us. We'll work fast and quiet. And there is another way out of there if we get into a jam."

Elle raised an eyebrow at me.

"Ready?" I asked Beatrice.

She nodded nervously.

"We'll take everything we can back with us," Logan reassured her. "You'll have time to sort it out at Witch Wood," he said confidently.

Taking the lead, I moved down the walkway back to the scene where my entire life had fallen apart. I pushed open the door to the lab. An undead body lay on the ground on the other side of the door. Putting my shoulder on the door, I gave it a hard shove and moved it aside. It was dark inside. The sunlight just barely passed into the space from the door outside.

"Layla," Logan whispered. I turned to see he was holding out a flashlight.

I took the light and snapped it on, scanning around the room. Nothing was left alive inside. I was suddenly very glad that Will and Tom had not come. Kiki, Summer, and Ethel—at least what was left of them—lay on the floor. Worse, so much worse, was the fact that while Kiki and Summer were gone, Ethel wasn't. When the flashlight shone on her, she turned and looked at me. She was nothing more than a husk. The lower half of her body had been eaten, and one of her arms had been ripped off. There were massive bites taken from her face.

"There," Logan said, pointing to Ethel.

"Yeah, she knows," Kellimore said softly as he set his hand on my arm. "You want me—"

"No," I said, crossing the room toward her.

"One of her people, right?" I heard Elle whisper to Kellimore.

He must have nodded since I didn't hear him respond.

I knelt beside Ethel.

"Ethel?" I whispered, knowing already that she was gone. Whatever Jamie and Elizabeth and the others were, Ethel was not one. I pulled out my boot dagger with the doe on the pommel. I closed my eyes, bracing myself, then put her out of her misery.

A soft hand touched my shoulder. "You okay?" Kellimore asked.

I nodded, inhaling deeply, then rose. Anger swelled in me once more. The next time I saw a fox, I was going to make a scarf out of its hide.

Another flashlight clicked on behind me. Logan and Beatrice were looking through the notes on the doctor's lab table. I stood looking down at the bodies of the ones I loved. I knew they would be here, but I hadn't been prepared for the grief and anger. My body shook with rage. I'd loved them like they were my own family, and I had failed them.

"This is amazing," Beatrice whispered. "I can see what she was doing."

I panned the flashlight around. The beam of light caught the doctor's white lab coat on the floor. While the edge of the coat was still white, the rest was stained with blood. Elizabeth had taken massive bites out of the doctor's face and body. But she had not devoured her. There was a scalpel sticking out of her eye. Had Elizabeth killed her or someone else?

"Jamie? James?"

"The doc," Kellimore said.

I nodded. How much I hated her. She had killed the man I loved. Perhaps she had a plan, but it wasn't one she'd shared with Jamie or anyone else. She'd used Jamie, made him her guinea pig without his permission. She deserved to die like this. Now I could only hope that what she'd learned, what she knew, wouldn't die with her.

"What's that?" Kellimore said, reaching out to take my hand gently, moving the beam of light toward the doctor's lab coat. There, inside the fabric, something glimmered.

Moving closer, I knelt and pulled the bloody coat away from the body to investigate. Inside the coat pocket, I found three syringes and a tiny notepad filled with the doctor's handwriting.

"Beatrice?" I called.

When she joined us, I passed her the notepad.

Kellimore studied the syringes closely. "The doc wanted to give me a shot for my headache."

I shook my head. "No, she wanted to infect you, just like she did to Jamie."

"Infect me?" he said, frowning. He stared at the syringes then back at the doctor's corpse.

"She infected Jamie on purpose. But I think...I think she did it because she believed she had a cure. A human trial," I said, shaking my head. "We got overrun before she could give him the antidote," I said then handed the syringes to Beatrice.

Beatrice looked closely at them. "They aren't the same. The liquid inside this one is different. We'll need to grab a microscope," she told Logan.

"Of course," Logan said.

"I didn't know she'd done that to Jamie," Kellimore said.

"Me either," Elle chimed in. "She was always a bitch, but I didn't think she could do something like that."

I cast a glance down at her body. Weird science. I shook my head and tried not to think too much, to feel too much.

Jamie had trusted her, and he'd paid for it with his life.

"Jamie? James?"

Nothing.

"I...I need a minute," I said. "I'll go scout around a little. I'll be back."

"You sure?" Kellimore asked, a worried expression crossing his face. "The undead are in the building."

Elle set her hand on his shoulder, passing him a knowing glance. Kellimore nodded and didn't say another word.

I turned and left the lab, careful to close the door behind me. My mind felt like it was crashing in on itself. After all we had survived, how could I just lose Jamie like this?

"Jamie? Where are you?"

Stepping back out onto the campus green, I looked all around. One undead man, who I suddenly realized had once been among the college survivors—until the kitsune came—shambled aimlessly across the lawn. His leg broken, he dragged it behind him as he moved slowly.

"Jamie? Can you hear me?"

There was no reply. I wasn't going to have enough time. Tristan would, no doubt, rush us back with the materials as quickly as he could. Before then, I needed to find Jamie. I decided to make a quick perimeter sweep.

Moving quickly and being as covert as possible, I ran across the campus green. My eyes searching everywhere, I passed through the grotto toward the picnic pavilions. I met with two of the shuffling undead who were easy pickings. But I didn't see Jamie anywhere.

"Jamie! Jamie, where are you?"

From under a pavilion, I looked across the campus lawn toward the large oak tree. If Jamie had seen us go through the portal, he would have known we were long gone. He wouldn't have stayed here waiting. But where would he go?

"*Jamie?*"

Dammit. He wasn't anywhere.

Frustrated, I turned and headed toward the front door of the college. If I was Jamie, where would I go? Back to the familiar? Back to some place where I could easily be found. Maybe the library, somewhere where he could keep an eye out for us?

I adjusted Buddie's bow and took a firmer grip on the shashka. The front door of the college was shattered. Glass littered the ground, glittering iridescently like diamonds. Bodies of the college people lay everywhere. One undead man lying just inside the building groaned. I thrust the blade of my shashka into his eye, silencing him.

The hallways were dimly lit. Had we missed anyone? Were there still any survivors left?

I passed by the student union. Many undead were still clustered inside. They rocked as they stood, but otherwise didn't move.

Stimulus. Response. At times, it seemed like the undead did nothing without some tantalizing stimulus in front of them. Perhaps the living and the dead weren't that different. After all, how many of us had mindlessly chased the rat race, not thinking, just moving forward. Stimulus. Response.

I moved toward the stairwell and headed slowly upward. The gates that blocked off the hallways were all down. Lying in the corner of the stairwell lay an undead woman whose leg was clearly broken. She hissed and bit at me. I made quick work of her before she grabbed the attention of the others.

Pausing at the second floor, I bent my ear to listen. There were more undead there. I could smell and hear them. Moving quickly and quietly, I wound my way up to the third floor. Just days before Cricket had led me down this very passageway. The photographs that had been hanging on the walls were now knocked off.

"Jamie? Are you here? Please come out. We've come back. We're going to find a cure. Jamie? James, I need you."

I was met with silence. Sadness swept over me. What if he was gone? What was I going to do then? If we found a cure, but I couldn't find him, what then?

But what if he was here?

And what if he wasn't safe?

Jamie would never hurt me, would he?

"Jamie?"

The third floor was completely silent save the sound of my heart thundering in my chest and the soft crunch of glass under my feet. The hallway was dark, but I didn't risk using the flashlight. My ears were tuned in to every sound. I got the shivering sensation that I was not alone. Somewhere in the shadows, someone or something was watching.

It was okay.

It was daytime.

It couldn't be vampires.

"Jamie?"

I moved slowly down the hallway to the library. The door was ajar, some fallen books haphazardly propping the door open. I slipped inside.

I scanned the wide, empty space.

"Hello?" I called softly, still overcome with the sense that someone was watching me. "Jamie? Jamie, are you here?"

Keeping my sword poised at the ready, I moved down the hallway toward the room where Jamie and I had shared our special night, where he had proposed to me. As I moved past each study room, I went slowly, carefully. There was nothing, no one.

But if there was nothing, why did I feel like there were eyes on me?

I finally came to the corner room.

My small heap of old clothing, and Jamie's, lay in the corner.

From back in the library, a stack of books slid to the ground with a thump. My heart slammed in my chest.

I stepped back into the hallway.

"Jamie? Is that you?"

Nothing.

"Who's there? Show yourself," I called as I moved down the hallway, my sword drawn.

As I rounded the bookshelves, the library door closed. Someone had moved the pile of books holding it open.

"Dammit," I whispered.

I paused for a moment.

I could see everywhere from here.

Just one last look.

I raced to the window and looked outside. I saw two of the shambling undead. I also saw Tristan racing in his shifted form across the lawn. He looked up at me. His ears were flat on his head, and he was moving fast. That did not look good.

I quickly scanned around. Nothing. No Jamie. He wasn't here anymore.

But someone was.

Moving quickly, I turned and headed back down the hallway. That awful sense of being watched was gone, and in its place, I felt a massive sense of urgency. I needed to get out of that building and fast. As I raced down the hallway, I heard something crash on the second floor below me.

And then I heard them.

I ran down the steps, pausing at the second floor. In the stained glass window, I saw someone's reflection. There was a flash of red hair and then I saw the undead moving toward me.

Dammit.

The kitsune were still here, and they had seen us.

I ran down to the first floor just as the undead began pouring out of the Student Union. My boots skidded to a stop. No. No. No.

When they spotted me, they groaned loudly and moved toward me. I turned and rushed out the front door. From Tristan's expression, I knew I wasn't the only one who realized we were compromised.

Moving quickly, I ran back toward the doctor's lab.

Then I heard them. Fox barks. A lot of them.

I was headed down the sidewalk when Tristan and the others came rushing out.

"Layla," Tristan called. "I saw—"

"I know. Me too. Listen."

A chorus of barks arose from the forest and inside the building.

"Shit," Elle said, "that sounds like...all of them."

"There's still a chance they don't know we came through at the stone. We need to try to make it back," Tristan said.

"Go, let's go," Logan said, taking Beatrice's hand.

We rushed out the front gate. The undead had started moving back toward the college.

"This way," Kellimore called, leading us a different route from where we'd come.

"Where are we going?" Tristan called.

"Come on," Kellimore yelled as we raced toward a large blue building a block or so away from the college. Fumbling in his pocket, Kellimore pulled out a ring of keys as he ran toward the building.

"What's this?" Tristan asked.

"My house," Kellimore replied.

He stuck a key into the garage door and heaved it open. There was a truck inside.

"In, in," Kellimore called, waving us toward the back of the truck. Moving fast, the others jumped in the back as I slid into the passenger seat. "Come on, Broomhilda," he said then clicked over the ignition.

The engine turned over, the truck coming to life.

"Yes!" Kellimore said. "Hold on."

Gunning the gas, he pulled the truck out onto the road and took off across town.

I shot him a bewildered glance.

"What?" he asked with a laugh. "I was prepared, just in case. And I was right."

"And apparently Tristan—"

"Need to know basis," Kellimore replied then pulled onto Main Street, the truck skidding as he turned sharply.

I slid the back window open. "What did you see?" I called to Tristan.

"The unseelie."

"They saw you?" Elle asked.

"Yes," Tristan replied. I could see he was clearly upset.

"They were in the building. They were waiting," I added.

"Hold on," Kellimore said then turned the truck across a baseball field toward the ridge. "There," he said, pointing toward a path in the woods not too far away.

I held on tight, watching in the back mirror. There was no sign of them.

"Jamie?" I called hopelessly once more.

Nothing.

Kellimore shoved the gears into four-wheel drive then set off down the path through the forest, dodging trees and bumping over rocks and fallen logs. Had my heart not been beating so hard in my chest, had I not been running for my life, I would have sworn I was back in Hamletville with Ian. As much refinement as life in the city had given me, wandering down the hallways of the Smithsonian museums, going to the symphony, and eating high-end food, I still secretly loved Hamletville's delights.

Kellimore turned the truck, guiding it through a low stream, and up a bank where it connected with a muddy dirt road. We whipped past a sign for the "Sons of Red Branch Campground." Moments later, pushing through ferns and overgrown brush, we arrived where we started.

But this time, we were not alone.

Three hawkish looking people surrounded the standing stone.

They were already there.

"Go easy," Tristan whispered as we slowly got out of the truck.

"Tristan," a tall, red-haired man called.

"And Logan," a red-haired woman, who looked much like the woman who'd led us into the trap at the Harpwind, purred.

"Oh yes, even the whclp is out," the man said with a laugh.

I cast a glance toward Logan whose expression was stormy.

Shaking, Beatrice crowded close to Elle who was clutching her knife and gun. Kellimore got out slowly, his weapon raised.

"Stand aside," Tristan said.

"No," said a very petite but stern-looking woman with deep red hair.

The kitsune man took a step forward.

I gave my shashka a spin then stepped between him and

Tristan.

"And you must be Layla," the man said then, grinning wickedly at me.

In the woods behind us, I heard the barks of foxes.

"You will move aside," I said to him.

"And why would I do that?"

"Because I told you to," I answered. "And because, even though your reinforcements are on their way, I can take your head before they get here. And my people have guns on you."

"Oh, yes. Humans and your weapons. You're no different than you were five hundred years ago, ready to chop the world apart," he said then walked toward me.

Arrogantly, he reached out as if he was going to brush my blade dismissively away.

Moving quickly, I circled the blade around his hand then slid it down his cheek, slicing open his flesh just a little, then let the blade come to rest on his neck.

The look of surprise on his face was priceless. He touched his cheek then looked at his bloody fingers.

"Kill her," the red-haired woman said.

"Go ahead," I taunted them. "Let's see you try." The image of Ethel's mangled body bubbled up in my mind, anger seething along with it. It was all I could do to keep from taking the kitsune's head right then.

"Lors," Tristan said then, intervening in the growing tension. "Enough of this. Mankind has died, and in their wake you have left the living dead. These humans have nothing to do with you. They are innocents. Leave them be. Your work is done."

The man looked at his bloody hand once more then glared at me. "We will not rest until they're all gone."

"Then you will have to fight through us to get to them,"

Logan answered.

"Well," Lors said, "then it will be as the humans used to say: two birds, one stone."

"And what will you do when the night fiends come? And the living undead? You sought to save this world, but instead you've turned it into a living grave," Tristan said.

"In time, all will come to right," the small woman said.

"And then what?" Tristan asked them.

"We'll take our place where we belong. Rulers of this realm. We'll come out of the mists and shadows."

"The mists and shadows are our world," Tristan said.

"You've chosen the wrong side, Tristan. When they are gone, we can all return," Lors said.

In a way, I knew the kitsune was right. If Tristan's people had been living in hiding all this time, our death would permit their return as well as the kitsune's.

"No," Logan told him. "Now tell your people to step aside."

"I can't do that," Lors answered.

The sound of barking was getting closer. One way or another, we needed to get through.

"You need to move," I said then. "This is your last warning."

"Layla," Tristan said, and I heard the cautioning in his voice.

"If she kills me, you know what will happen," Lors warned Tristan.

"Yes, we do," Logan answered. "The unseelie will lose their dread king, and the humans will have taken some vengeance."

"I've already broken you," Lors said then, looking down at me with his yellow eyes. "Why won't you just die?"

"It's not over yet," I whispered.

"Okay. Enough of this," the petite red-haired woman said, then moving quickly, she pulled a knife from her inner coat pocket and lobbed it at me.

"No!" Lors shouted.

I grabbed Lors, pulling him between me and the blade. The knife hit him in the shoulder.

Kellimore took aim at the petite red-haired woman and fired.

Startled, as if she couldn't believe such a thing could happen, her face froze, and then she crumpled dead onto the ground.

"No," the other woman screamed, and with a jerking movement, she shifted into a large fox and lunged at Elle. She bit Elle hard on the arm. With a scream, Elle dropped her gun.

"Go, Logan," I yelled. "Get Beatrice through!"

Logan grabbed Beatrice's hand, and they rushed toward the stone.

"No," Lors screamed, moving to stop them, but my quick blade on his neck gave him pause. He growled then cocked his head backward, smashing it into my face.

The moved dazed me, and I let him go.

"Layla," Kellimore called.

Lors then stepped back and pulled his own blade from his robes. It was a long, slim, razor-cut weapon. I'd never seen anything like it before.

Lors swung at me. "Do you think you can outmaneuver me, human?"

"I already have once," I said, my eyes flicking toward his cheek.

"Underestimated you," he said, swinging at me. "It won't happen again."

His moves were fast and fluid. Our swords clanged against

one another, and I felt the heavy shake of my blade, the vibration rippling through to my bones. He was vastly stronger than me, and his blade was made out of some strange, dense metal.

"Go, go," Tristan called to Elle and Kellimore, waving them both toward the stone.

"Not without Layla," Kellimore said. "She won't be able to get back alone."

Lors and I circled one another, steel clattering.

"Go," I yelled to them. "Tristan, go! Get them out of here."

There was a strange crackling sound, and when I looked back, I saw they were gone.

"So much for protecting his ward," Lors said, his blade clanging against mine.

"I'm not his ward," I said, kicking him hard in the gut, sending him stumbling backward.

The kitsune man caught his breath then lunged once more. He was good, but he over-relied on his height and strength. I moved quickly around him, trying to keep my breath even, my movements precise. Patience. That's what I always preached to my students. Size the opponent up, then be patient.

"Been awhile?" I asked Lors. "You look tired." Hoping to get him to talk, to wear himself out, I goaded him.

"Filthy human," he swore then came at me again.

Out of the corner of my eye, I could see that the first of his people had arrived. They slipped around the trees and through the brush, shifting into human form. They looked appalled at the sight before them.

"My lord," one of the females called, but Lors ignored her.

When our blades clattered against one another once more,

he pressed his weight against me. He was going to push me under.

"Give up," I whispered, pushing back against him with all my might. "Give up, and I'll spare you," I said.

"You?" he asked with a laugh. "In a minute, I'm going to have your pretty head. I'll take it as a trophy. You can sit on my table tonight and watch me at supper. And after, I'll feed your pretty face to the dogs."

"No," I said then. "Not today."

At that, I let go. Ducking low, I pulled my boot dagger out and shoved it hard into his chest, slipping the blade under the ribs toward the heart. His own weight played against him, driving the blade in deep. He toppled over me, onto the ground, then rolled, his hands clutching the dagger.

"You bitch," he gasped, glaring at me. Then his eyes went dim, and his hands fell away.

I reached down and pulled out my dagger. Stashing it back into my boot, I backed toward the stone then turned and waited.

The kitsune looked at one another in disbelief.

"Don't just stand there. Kill her," one of them called.

I waited.

A moment.

A moment more.

They rushed me.

I dipped into my pocket and pulled out two grenades. Activating them in sync, I tossed them into the crowd.

The kitsune paused, shocked expressions on their faces, as they saw what was coming. But it was too late.

As the grenades exploded, I set my hand on the stone and was swept away.

CHAPTER TWENTY
CRICKET

VELLA, ARIEL, AND I SAT ON THE FLOOR of the tower study at the top floor of Witch Wood estate. The tower, which jutted out from the main building, had windows on three sides. Ariel had tucked herself in along the window and was looking out.

"What ya looking at?" I asked her, turning away from Vella who was shuffling her cards.

"I'm watching Darius try to work a plow," she said with a grin. "I can *almost* hear him swearing from here."

"A plow?"

Ariel laughed. "Madame Knightly came in this morning and asked Tom, Will, Chase, and Darius to do some work. They could hardly say no, I guess."

"She's trying to keep them busy," Vella said absently.

Chase had been skittish all morning, annoyed that Vella had told him not to go. And Layla's people looked like they might go into the maze after her at any minute. "They were worried about Layla," I said, trying to hide the tremor in my voice. I was worried about Tristan, but no doubt Vella and Ariel knew that already.

Vella raised an eyebrow at me.

"What?" I asked innocently.

She smirked.

"They'll be back. Everything's going to be fine. I'm not worried a bit," I said then looked at Vella. "Okay, Vella. You've been playing with those cards all morning. So, is there going to be a cure or what?"

Ariel turned her attention to Vella. Apparently she'd been waiting for an answer as well.

Vella laid down her cards. "Nothing comes easy now."

"That's a lot of swords," Ariel observed.

Vella nodded.

"Can you see anything?" I asked, glancing at the cards. Scene after scene depicted battles. I didn't need to be a tarot reader to know the future looked dark.

"There is light, but much darkness comes before it."

"What should we do?" Ariel asked. "We need to find somewhere safe. I don't care where. Are we safe here?"

Vella frowned then looked at the cards. "Yes and no," she said then picked up a card I hadn't seen before.

"What's that?" I asked. The image depicted a woman seated on a chair wearing blue robes.

"*The High Priestess*," she said. "She's a woman sitting between the worlds, standing between the veil of the known and the unknown, using her intuition and magic as her guide."

"Madame Knightly?" I asked.

Vella set the card down then lifted, one by one, others she had drawn: *The Queen of Swords*, which I knew was for Layla, a card with a lion on it titled *Strength*, and another one with a big wheel on it called *The Wheel of Fortune*. She set the wheel at the top, and underneath, placed the queen, the lion, and the priestess. She nodded slowly then answered, "No, not Madame Knightly."

"Then who?" I asked.

"Her," Ariel answered, pointing out the window.

I followed Ariel's gaze. Outside, Amelia was walking toward the rose garden, a black cat following alongside her.

CHAPTER TWENTY-ONE

AMELIA

I LOOKED UP AT THE LATE AFTERNOON SKY. They'd been gone for hours. Hours. I'd spent the entire day in the kitchen churning out homemade pasta and trying not to think about the fact that Logan and the others were still gone, that Mom had somehow communicated with Layla, and that my magical powers seemed to be growing in some weird way that I didn't understand.

Zoey had been chatty, too chatty. At some point, I realized she was talking just to talk. I had no idea what she'd been saying. It was just about that point when Madame Knightly entered the kitchen.

"Amelia," Madame Knightly said. "Why don't you come with me? And Zoey, won't you be a dear and take the boys something to drink. Oh my," she said then, looking at the row upon row of pasta we had hanging on an old clothes rack drying. "Looks wonderful," she said with a nod then motioned to me.

I smiled at Zoey, pulled off the apron I was wearing, then went outside with Madame Knightly.

"You look worried, Amelia," Madame Knightly said.

"Yes. Logan and the others have been gone too long."

"Oh, not to worry, Tristan is one of our best. He'll see to them." With a blink of light, she shifted into the form of

Bastet once more and trotted beside me, leading me toward the rose garden.

I shook my head, still trying to get over the sight of it, then followed along. The rose garden had been a tangled mess, but earlier this spring, while the roses were still sleeping, I'd attacked the garden. With Madame Knightly's guidance, and having read at least a dozen books on roses, I was able to get all the roses trimmed and staked. The vines were now coming back to life. New green leaves grew and small buds were just forming. I'd been excited to see the garden in bloom once more, but now my thoughts were distracted. It was like, at Witch Wood, we'd just been able to turn off the world and go on living. Out of sight, out of mind. The dark world was still there. We'd just been ignoring it.

With Layla's arrival we'd been reminded that we really weren't safe, nor were we alone. Didn't we have some responsibility for helping those who still lived? It was hardly fair for us to go on living behind enchanted walls. Except, *enchanted* wasn't exactly the right word for it.

At the center of the rose garden was a large reflecting pool. All around the pool were marble statues, most of which depicted Greek or Roman gods. There were a few, however, I didn't recognize. When we reached the image of a goddess I assumed to bc Demeter, Madame Knightly took form once more.

She smiled at me, smoothed her dress, and then looked me over. She reached out and adjusted a button on my shirt then righted my collar.

"Very well then," she said and took my hand. "Here we go, Amelia." She set our hands on the foot of the goddess.

What happened then was unbelievable. I felt like I'd suddenly got caught in a wind turbine. I could feel a rush of air as I was sucked into a tunnel of light, and then, a moment later, I found myself standing in a grassy field. It took me a moment to steady myself.

"Madame Knightly?"

She smiled at me then linked her arm with mine. "Come along," she said then we walked toward a stream nearby. A man stood looking into the water.

The moment I saw him, I realized he was not human. The light around him glimmered opalescent. He turned and looked at us.

"Madame," he said, bowing his head. "This is an unexpected visit."

"Yes. How I do hate the gates. Of course you know Amelia," she said, turning to me.

"I…I…hi," I stammered.

The man chuckled. "Amelia, I am Obryn, the leader of my people."

I dropped the best curtsey I could muster. "Pleased to meet you."

He smiled.

"I've come to ask if you've made a decision," Madame Knightly said, her voice sounding pert and mildly irritated.

Obryn's expression turned serious. "We must not interfere more. Especially not now."

"Not now?" Madame Knightly asked.

"Lors has been killed."

Madame Knightly looked shocked. "How?"

"Layla."

Madame Knightly nodded. "The unseelie brought it on themselves."

"Yes," Obryn agreed. "But we must not be in the middle when it ends."

"You are right," Madame Knightly said with a sigh.

Obryn turned to me. "The humans may not live among us, that is true, but I'm not saying that they shouldn't seek out a place for themselves. Does she have the aptitude you suspected?"

"Yes."

"Then time is of the essence," he said then passed Madame Knightly a knowing look.

"As you wish," she said, then took my hand.

Once more, I felt a strange rush. This time, as we hurled back through the strange in-between space, I smelled death. The scent of decay perfumed the air. The awful scent was so heavy that I could taste it in my mouth. A moment later, we appeared once more in the rose garden.

In the far off distance, I heard a familiar voice.

"Amelia! Amelia? Where's Amelia?" Logan called. I could hear the panic in his voice.

"Logan?" I turned to Madame Knightly. "They're back. Something's wrong."

She nodded. "I'm all right. Go on ahead."

I raced across the lawn. My mind reeled with what I had just seen, but beyond that, I saw Tristan and Elle emerge from the maze. Tristan was holding on to Elle. Blood was dripping down her arm.

"What happened?" I called as I ran toward them.

"She was bit by an animal, one of the kitsune," Logan explained.

"Let's get her inside," I said. "It will be okay. We'll get you cleaned up."

"One of those people bit me," Elle exclaimed.

"Don't worry about her. I got her for you," Kellimore told Elle.

"Thanks," Elle said through gritted teeth.

I held her arm gently as we led her inside.

"Where's Layla?" Kellimore asked.

I cast a glance backward. They were all back…except one.

CHAPTER TWENTY-TWO

LAYLA

I GROANED AS I FOUND MYSELF FACE DOWN in the dirt once more. This was getting old. I closed my eyes and listened. In the distance, I heard the call of a mourning dove. Otherwise, it was totally silent. Where were the others?

I sat up to find I was in the woods…somewhere. It was very foggy. I rose, grabbed my sword, and looked around.

Not daring to speak for fear of what might be nearby, I wandered through the fog. It was so dense that I could barely see two feet in front of me. I held my sword at the ready just in case.

Finally, in the far off distance, I heard the clatter of metal.

Moving forward, mindful that there were all manner of creatures out there that wanted me dead, I went slowly. In the looming distance, I was able to make out the shape of a very large building. A barn? I walked slowly toward it, and as I did so, the air around me began to clear.

Yes, it was a barn.

Near the barn was a tall chain-linked fence.

Beyond, as the fog lifted, I saw something quite unbelievable.

Home.

I was home.

I stood staring at my grandmother's cabin, her barn. I was

back in Hamletville.

Sliding the sword into its scabbard, I climbed the fence and dropped onto the property. My SUV was still parked in the driveway. Everything was exactly as I had left it the day we'd gone to the Harpwind.

I looked around for the source of the noise, finding that a piece of scrap metal had blown against the fence and was slapping against the side every time the wind blew.

How had I gotten here? Everyone else must have gone back to Witch Wood. Why had I come home?

I crossed the lawn to the front door, dug the key out of the old silk flower decoration hanging by the door, and then went inside.

Even though it was daytime, the light was dim inside the house. Thin slants of light shone through the windows, catching motes of dust in its rays. How very strange. The whole place was exactly as I left it. All the little decorations Kira and Susan had made covered the walls, crayon artwork depicting rainbows and flowers. The only good thing I'd managed to do so far was keep Kira and Susan alive. It was a promise I'd made to their mother from the start, that I'd keep them safe, and I'd made good on that promise.

I sat down on the couch and pulled out the engagement ring. Blood had smeared across the band. I wiped it off with the edge of my shirt then slid the ring on once more. Then, I let it in. I'd been trying to stay strong, to think straight. I needed to make decisions about our next move, to decide what to do, who to trust. I never let it in.

I had gone back for him, but he was gone. Had the disease taken him? Was he like the other decaying undead now? Or was he elsewhere, lost to the illness that had swept over him? I put my head in my hands and wept hard. How had this happened?

He was gone. I felt like someone had reached into my chest and torn my heart in half. Worse, if there was a cure, how would I ever even find Jamie? He wasn't at Claddagh-Basel, at least not that I could discover. I could go back, but the kitsune were watching that place. It wasn't safe.

At least for now, Witch Wood was secure. We could try to find a way to keep mankind alive. Maybe there was a chance. And if not, if we failed, at least I'd found a safe place for Susan and Kira. After all, with the kitsune still hunting us, there was nowhere else for us to go.

"Pssh," someone said then.

I looked up to find my grandmother sitting in her favorite chair.

"Grandma?"

"My Layla, your head is a mess," she said.

"I—"

"And your hair too. Clean up a bit before you head back."

"I don't know how to get back."

"The mists, my girl. The thin places. Focus on where you want to go then walk."

"That must be how I got here," I said absently.

"And now you must return. You have work to finish before you can come home."

"Come home?"

"Of course. It's nearly time. But first, you must help your friends."

"This place isn't safe. The vampires—"

"Yes, the strigoi found their way here. But there are not so many."

"How many?"

"Eh," she said then shrugged. *"Three haunt Hamletville at night."*

I frowned.

"It's better to be slapped with the truth than kissed with a lie, isn't

it?" she said with a smile. *"Three is nothing for you, my girl."*

"We have other enemies. Others who want us dead."

She nodded. *"The dark leshi. I have seen."*

I shook my head. "The world is too dangerous now. We... we don't have a place in this world anymore."

"Then perhaps it's time to get a new one."

"A new what?"

"World."

I sighed heavily and leaned back into the couch, closing my eyes. "Jamie," I whispered. "I lost him. I can't find him anywhere. I need to find him. Have you seen..." I began, opening my eyes, but when I looked up, Grandma was gone.

"Grandma?"

There was nothing.

I sighed deeply then rose and went to my bedroom. The place felt so foreign to me. Sitting on my bed, I ran my brush through my hair, pulling it back into a ponytail. I then rose and went into Frenchie's room. I pulled out a duffle and stuffed it with clothes for the girls and some of their favorite stuffed animals. I turned and went back outside.

The mist was thicker than ever.

I locked the door, stuffing the key back into the planter. At the back of the property, I passed the barn, and headed toward the fence, but the mist grew heavy all around me and the fence never appeared.

I closed my eyes. *Witch Wood,* I thought then walked forward, my mind on Frenchie, Kira, Susan, Will, Tom, and the others. The image of Kellimore's smiling face and light blue eyes came to mind. *Witch Wood.*

As I walked forward, the mists slowly began to clear. Once again, I heard the sound of a mourning dove. But this time, I found myself surrounded by tall hedges. I was back in the maze. I scanned the horizon, and just above the tall shrubbery, I saw the turrets of Witch Wood. I threaded through the maze, taking a couple of wrong turns, before I finally found myself back on the grassy lawn.

Cricket exited the house and made her way toward me.

"And here we thought you'd gone off to Oz," she said with a grin. "They're inside now arguing about where you are and what to do. Kellimore's got about every gun loaded and is twisting Tristan's arm to go back for you."

"Sorry to worry everyone. I got kind of...lost," I said then eyed her over, realizing that she already had her machete belted, her wrench in her hand, and a pistol in her back pocket. "Thank you," I said, motioning to her armaments. Clearly, she was planning to come back for me as well. My heart swelled with gratitude.

"Like I told you, gotta save the living."

I smiled at her. "Is Elle okay?"

"Nasty bite, but Amelia and Beatrice got her patched up. Mostly she's just cranky. But they have antibiotics and pain killers, so she'll be okay. Tristan said there was no sign of Jamie."

I shook my head.

"I'm sorry."

"Yeah," I said then exhaled heavily. "Yeah. Better go in before Kellimore does something rash."

Cricket laughed. "Him? Never."

I smiled.

Grandma said it was almost time to come home. It wasn't going to be easy, but she was right. I was done with this world. It was time to do something new, something different. It was time to find a new way to survive. And the last time Grandma had told me to come home, she'd saved my life.

CHAPTER TWENTY-THREE

LAYLA

"OH, THANK GOD," FRENCHIE SAID as soon as I entered.

Everyone was standing in the foyer.

"Layla? What happened?" Will, who was holding two shotguns, asked.

"I made a stop to go shopping," I said then handed Frenchie the bag. At first, she looked confused. She stared at the bag then at me, her eyes wide.

"Layla?" she whispered, her voice filled with confusion.

"What is it?" Tom asked.

"This belongs to the girls. We left it in Hamletville."

Everyone looked at me.

"When I went in through the doorway, it took me somewhere else," I said then turned to Tristan and Madame Knightly. "Is it supposed to work like that?"

Tristan looked thoughtful. "Not usually."

"The mist playing tricks. Especially if your mind was busy with something," Madame Knightly said.

"So can we use these doors to leap anywhere?" Cricket asked.

"No," Madame Knightly said. "Each doorway leads to another thin place on the human plane. It's easy, however, to get lost in the in-between spaces."

"Are you all right?" Kellimore asked.

I nodded.

"See, nothing to worry about for now," Madame Knightly said. "Let's put the weapons back into the gentlemen's parlor, shall we?"

Tristan nodded, then waved to the others to follow him.

"Layla, thank you," Frenchie said. "The girls will be so happy."

I nodded. "Welcome. I need to see Beatrice."

"Cricket, be a dear and take her, would you? I'll go check on dinner," Madame Knightly said then turned toward the kitchen.

Cricket and I went back to the old library. Inside, Beatrice, Logan, and Zoey were pouring over the notes we had recovered, papers and books spread out all over the place.

"Cricket, how is Elle?" Beatrice asked.

"Asleep."

"Did we find what we needed?" I asked Beatrice.

"I think so. I'm just looking now. Logan, hand me that petri dish. Zoey, I need more light."

"On it, Miss B," Zoey said.

"Can I help?" I asked.

Beatrice shook her head as she flipped through the pages of the doctor's notebook. "Um. No. Thank you. Logan and Zoey were two of my best students. I'll manage."

"Who knew paying attention in chemistry was going to come in so handy," Zoey said as she adjusted the flashlight. "Well, except Logan," she said then frowned at him.

"Sorry, Zoey. I wasn't permitted to say anything. You know that."

"I do, but I still don't like it."

"Okay you two, shut it," Beatrice said, concentrating. "I

have more work to do here, Layla. But I'll be sure to let you know as soon as I unravel anything."

I nodded.

"If you need anything, let us know," Cricket said then motioned for me to come with her. "I like those kids. And Beatrice seems all right," Cricket told me when we were out of earshot.

I frowned. "I hardly trust myself to form an opinion about anyone anymore."

"You mean Doctor Gustav."

"Yes. And before that too."

"Well, I knew Doctor Gustav for months, but I never thought she'd do something like that. I don't know. This new world changes people. Some for better, some for worse. I'm sorry for what happened. Can I do anything for you?"

I shook my head.

"All right then," she said. "I'm going to check on Elle again. That girl, Amelia, has a healer's touch. She worked on that wound, not even touching it, but after that Elle felt better."

"Worked on it how?"

"She said something about auras."

I nodded.

"Glad you made it back in one piece. See you around," Cricket said, and with a wave, she headed upstairs.

I stood in the foyer of the opulent estate. A massive chandelier hung overhead. There was a mosaic on the floor in the shape of a large tree. It was a beautiful place. Much like the Harpwind, under any other circumstances, I would have loved being there. But that was then and this was now. Now, I was visiting such a grand manor under the protection of the seelie. My friends were dead. My world was dead. And it was time to face the truth. Jamie was dead.

"Layla?" Kellimore called softly.

I looked away from the lovely old chandelier toward him. I hadn't realized it, but tears were rolling down my cheeks.

"Sorry, I didn't see you," I said, dashing the hot tears away.

Kellimore frowned sympathetically. "Can I do anything for you?"

"No. It's just so much loss," I said, unable to hold back the tears anymore. I breathed hard, and the tears flowed in earnest.

Crossing the room, Kellimore gently wrapped his arms around me.

"I know," he whispered. "I know. My family. My sister. My home. I know," he said, holding me tightly as I wept.

It felt so good to have someone's strong arms around me, to be weak, to let go of all the pretense and just feel the sadness that wanted to flood over me. I'd lost nearly everything. And it wasn't over yet.

"Going on seems so pointless," I whispered.

"We're going to make it. We are survivors. All of us here. We'll find a way. Don't give up now."

I inhaled a deep, shuddering breath. "Yeah."

Kellimore laughed. "That wasn't very convincing. Look at me," he said, pulling back. "See this?" he said, motioning to the scar on his face. "We were locked down in a bar, me and a dozen people from Ulster. Zombies were busting through the door. I held them back, let the others escape. Everyone lived that day. But when the glass on the door broke, I got this. Damned near lost my eye," he said then shook his head. "But I knew I couldn't give up. Even if I died, it didn't matter. I had to save the people around me. You and I are a lot alike. And people like us don't give up."

I looked at the rough and angry scar down the side of his face. All the scars I carried were on the inside. But I carried them. Kellimore was right.

"I did take out most of the kitsune with grenades before I made the jump," I said with a half-smile, wiping the last of my tears off my cheeks.

"There you go," he said then grinned. "You just need some rest. Tomorrow is another day, Layla...Layla what?"

"Petrovich."

"Layla Petrovich," he said then nodded. "Get some rest, Layla Petrovich. No doubt Swamp Thing and some mummies will be by tomorrow for a good ass kicking."

I nodded. "See you later then," I said, motioning to the stairs.

He nodded.

"And Kellimore, thank you."

He grinned, as if he was cooking up something smart-assed to say, but then stopped himself. "You're welcome," he said with a soft smile then turned and headed back to the parlor.

Feeling confused and surprisingly happy, I went upstairs. I was pretty sure I'd spotted a small smoking room on the second floor, and if I remembered right, it had a bar. With any luck, there would be vodka. Because with a head swimming around in a mess of emotions like this, there was hardly anything better to do than drink.

CHAPTER TWENTY-FOUR

AMELIA

IT WAS SOMETIME AFTER MIDNIGHT when I went downstairs. I'd tossed and turned all night, unable to shake my mother from my mind. She'd been at our house all this time. She was dead, that was clear, but if so, how had Layla heard her? I always knew the world was full of things just beyond human perception, but the truth was deeper than I ever expected.

I pulled my robe tight around me. It was weird to sleep in one of the upstairs bedrooms. I'd grown so used to bunking in the parlor that taking one of the rooms felt like I was overreaching. Stupid, I knew. Nonetheless, sleep didn't come easy to me there. I was about to take my spot on the chaise once more when I heard voices echo down the hallway. Curious, I followed the sound to discover that there was still a light on in the library.

"This one," I heard Logan say.

Beatrice muttered something incomprehensible. Had they been working the whole time? I'd taken them some food at dinner time, but then spent the rest of the night sitting at Elle's bedside while she slept. So far, so good. There was no infection, and what little darkness wanted to swell around her injury, I'd kept at bay. By the time I finally headed to bed, the area around the bite was glimmering with gold and brilliant white light. Her body was healing itself.

I entered the library to find Logan poring over some notes while Beatrice eyed the microscope.

"Still awake?" I asked groggily.

Logan smiled. "And I could really use a Starbucks."

"So, Frappuccino? With or without a side of pixie dust?"

"Very funny," he replied with a yawn.

"How's it coming?"

"Well, took us about three hours to figure out some of the equations here, and make our way through this handwriting, but—"

"But what I'm seeing here is amazing. And horrifying," Beatrice said, shaking her head.

She sat back in her seat. "The flu shot caused a reaction. It's like someone set a bomb to detonate inside us. The minute it brushed up against a flame—"

"Boom," Logan said quietly.

"Everyone who was immunized became ticking time bombs."

"Did that doctor find a cure?"

Beatrice picked up a syringe. "Here," she said, gazing at the golden-colored liquid in the vial. "But I don't know if it works. I heard what she did to Layla's fiancé. It was wrong, but she was trying to get a human trial to test this. That was the only way to be sure. Her notes show that the animal trials were successful."

"We can't test it," Logan said, shaking his head.

"What about…" I said then paused, not wanting to say it, but at the same time, daring to hope. "What about on one of the undead? Could we test it on one of them?"

Beatrice shook her head. "They're so rotted. Their organs are no longer intact."

"No, not all of them," I said, casting a glance at Logan.

"Oh, Amelia," Logan said, catching my drift. "Are you sure?"

I nodded. "If there is a chance this might restore her, I'll try anything."

"We'll need Layla to come with us to...communicate," Logan said.

I nodded.

"I'm sorry, who?" Beatrice asked.

"My mother. She was infected. You'll see, she's not like the others. She's something different now. We can try it on her."

Beatrice let out a deep breath.

"We need to get more supplies, things from the medical center, if we want to make more antidote," Logan said.

"Back into town," Beatrice said. "That place we went today. Those creatures. We can't let them find us here. If they do..."

"We'll be safe. Brighton isn't even on their radar," Logan reassured her.

"I hope you're right," Beatrice said.

She was right to hope, because when I looked at the energy surrounding Logan, I knew he was lying. But it hardly mattered. I had a chance to save my mother. Nothing filled me with greater joy.

Goddess Mother, please let it work. Please give me my mother back.

CHAPTER TWENTY-FIVE

AMELIA

THE NEXT MORNING, MADAME KNIGHTLY LISTENED PATIENTLY as Beatrice, Logan, and I explained our plan. The others looked skeptical. Cricket's brows furrowed so hard that I was afraid she was going to get a headache. I eyed Layla who said nothing, simply listened. When we were done, Madame Knightly adjusted her dress, then rose.

"This is your world. All you can do is try," she said. "Tristan will assist you," she added, nodding to him, then she left.

"Right then," Tristan said. "We'll head into town in two small groups. Logan will lead one group to the medical center to get supplies. Cricket and Chase, can you help him?"

"Anything for you, darlin'," Cricket said with a grin.

Chase nodded.

"Zoey, you mind going with them too? You know the town."

"Sure."

"Beatrice, I'll take you, Amelia, and Layla."

"And me," Kellimore said.

"Me too," Will added.

Layla frowned.

"Darius and Tom will be here," Will told her, "and these ladies are no slouches. You're going to need more muscle, just in case."

"Vella? What do you think?" Tristan asked.

She shrugged. "Everything we do now poses risk."

"That's comforting," Chase said.

Vella smiled in apology, opening her hands wide.

"All right," Layla relented.

"Let's ammo up," Kellimore said.

Everyone headed to the gentlemen's parlor to grab some guns.

Zoey came over to me. "You going to be okay?"

I shook my head. "No, but we have to try."

"What if it works?" Zoey said.

"What if it doesn't?" I replied, but then Zoey took me by the arms and looked me in the eyes.

"What if it works?" she asked again, this time in a low voice. "You have no idea how she'll be. It might be bad, Amelia. It might be really bad. You need to prepare yourself."

"I..." I began, but then I felt my eyes welling with tears. "I know. I'll...I'll just handle it."

"Love you, girl," she said, pulling me close.

"Love you, too."

"Don't get your hopes up, okay?"

"Okay."

"Now, let me go see where Chase went," Zoey said with a wink.

"Chase, huh?"

Zoey smiled.

"There's something we can get our hopes up about."

"A girl can dream," Zoey replied with a wink then followed the others.

I went outside. I cast a glance toward the greenhouse. I needed to water the seedlings when I got back. Just because our routine had gotten turned upside down didn't mean we shouldn't keep after our work here. After all, with this many people in the house, food would eventually run short. From now on, we needed to start rationing just in case.

I felt a warm little body rub against my shin. Bastet.

"I know," I said. "I'll be careful."

The cat meowed at me.

"And when I get back, I'd like to talk to you about what Obryn said."

Once again, the cat meowed. I reached down and scratched her ears.

"Ready?" I heard Chase call as the others came outside. Beatrice, I noticed, looked decidedly pale.

I looked at Bastet. "Be back soon," I said then joined the others. And with a lot of luck, maybe, just maybe, I'd have my mother with me.

CHAPTER TWENTY-SIX

CRICKET

"TURN HERE," ZOEY SAID, pointing down a side street. The ride into Brighton had been a quiet one. The fact that Amelia had offered her mother up as a test subject moved us all. What could we do but hope that, in the end, we'd find an answer. What the doc had done was wrong, but I understood why she'd done it. We all did, including Layla. But that didn't make it right.

"There," Zoey said, directing me toward the Brighton Car Cabana. Row after row of used cars sat untouched. A colorful rainbow banner lay on the ground. All the cars were covered in dust.

"All right," I said, slipping out of the driver's seat. "We'll find something here. Or we'll walk."

"Are you sure?" Tristan asked, touching me gently on the chin.

"Of course," I replied. "Don't worry about me. I've got my wrench."

Tristan smiled at me, placed a light kiss on my lips, and then slid into the driver's seat.

Chase, Zoey, and Logan hopped out of the back of the truck.

"Careful, girl," Zoey called to Amelia.

"You too," Amelia said, casting a glance at Logan who

waved to her.

After a moment, they drove off.

"Well, what shall we grab? Daddy always wanted a nice Cadillac. Convertible? Hummer? How about that Corvette?"

Chase grinned, shaking his head.

"There's some trucks and SUVs," Logan said, pointing.

"Trucks, trucks, and more trucks. I don't think I was ever meant to drive a convertible," I said with a sigh.

Zoey laughed. "You definitely don't strike me as the convertible type. What did you do before things went to shit?"

"Carnival. Ride operator," I said, trying to hide the nagging feelings of both pride and shame that wanted to let loose in my chest.

"Oh. That's badass. I bet that was a fun job, traveling all over like that."

I loved her so much in that moment, I wanted to give her a hug. "Yeah, me and my daddy traveled the whole country."

"What was your favorite place? Best carnival?"

"Pensacola. White beaches. Blue water. Good times and tan lines."

Zoey laughed.

"What about you? You were about done with school, right? What were you going to do?"

Zoey shrugged. "I don't know. Become a writer, maybe."

"You can still do that, ya know."

"Seems pointless now. I mean, what's there to write about? Who wants to read a book about the zombie apocalypse?"

"It would be great. *The Battle of Claddagh-Basel. The War Against the Kitsune.* Make sure you mention how much ass I kicked."

Zoey laughed. "Yeah? Well, we'll see."

"It's a whole new world," I told her, setting my arm across

her shoulders. "And you know the best thing?"

She raised an eyebrow at me.

"I bet you're the best writer on the whole planet."

At that, she laughed.

Logan grinned. "Shall we go inside? See if we can find some keys?"

"Let's go slow," Chase said. "Brighton's residents didn't get far."

"This guy, Ray, owned the place. He'll have it all locked up," Zoey said.

We headed across the parking lot, stopping when we got to the showroom.

"Is that Ray?" Logan asked.

Pressed against the glass was a middle-aged man in a heavy state of decay, his flesh torn all around his neck. The funny thing was, he was still wearing a short-sleeved button-up shirt and a tie.

"Yep."

"See anyone else?" Chase asked.

Zoey shook her head.

"Let's double check," Chase said then went to the window and rapped on the glass. We waited a few minutes. There was no one else inside, but in the parking lot, I heard that same old groan. I looked behind me to see an undead woman dressed in what was left of a brown suit, and another man dressed similar to Ray, coming toward us.

"Got her," I said, pulling out my machete. The smell coming off her reminded me of the time Daddy was so tired that he forgot to bring in the groceries from the car. Everything was still there when he remembered two days later. It took us a month to air the car out, and the upholstery smelled like spoiled milk for a long time after that. When I got a good look at the woman, I saw there were large black flies crawling all over her face and maggots tumbling out of her open mouth.

I dropped the knife on the center of her head. It took me a good wiggle to get the blade loose.

I turned to see Zoey swipe at the man with a baseball bat. When he fell, she bashed his head in.

"Ray," Logan called, tapping on the glass to distract the undead man.

"Stay back," Chase said, motioning to Zoey. He smashed open the glass, unlocked the door, then swung it open wide.

The undead man, no longer distracted by Logan, came stumbling out. I bashed him in the head with my wrench then stabbed him through the eye with my knife.

"Sorry, Ray," Zoey said as we all stepped around him and went inside.

"Oh man, look at that," Chase said, crossing the showroom to run his hand along the curves of a silver and black 1970s Mustang Fastback. "Come on Cricket, please?"

"You kidding me? The engine sound alone will have half the zombies following us back to Witch Wood. Better find yourself a Prius."

"Ugh," Chase said with a shake of the head. "You just stay here, bae," he said, patting the hood of the Mustang. "I'll be back for you when Cricket's not looking."

Zoey stepped around the counter. "Key rack is empty. Just the Jeep and the Mustang," she said, referring to the two cars in the showroom as she lifted two sets of keys.

"Jeep it is then," I said, scanning the windows. "There," I added, pointing to the locks on the showroom window. Logan and I headed to the window, unlocked the glass, and with a hard shove, opened a space to drive the Jeep out.

"Here," Zoey said, tossing the Jeep keys to Chase.

"Thanks."

"Nothing I can steal is good enough for you."

"Remind me to rob a bank for you later."

"Sure. We could use the kindling," she replied with a grin.

Chase popped the hood on the Jeep, fiddling around underneath, then slipped into the driver's seat and started the engine. Logan and I hopped into the back of the Wrangler as Zoey slid into the passenger seat. She pulled the sticker off the window.

"We owe Ray twenty-five thousand," Zoey said.

"And a new head. We'll just put them both on a tab," I replied.

With a laugh, we headed off.

CHAPTER TWENTY-SEVEN

LAYLA

THE TRUCK SLIPPED QUICKLY through town toward Amelia's house. I could see from the expression on her face that she was trying to hold back her tears. I didn't blame her. If this didn't work, her mother would be lost forever.

"That's my place," Beatrice said, pointing to a pretty little cottage that sat on the end of a small pond.

"Do you want to stop?" Kellimore asked her.

She shook her head, then gazed back down at the bundle she was carrying.

"Reminds me of Hamletville," Will said, looking around. "A mess though," he added as we drove past a burned-out car. In the car after it, two undead were still locked inside.

"No one even had time to run. Everyone just panicked," Beatrice said.

The truck slowed as we turned into Amelia's driveway.

Will helped Beatrice out of the truck, and we went inside. Once more, Amelia set her hand on the large oak tree out front. This time, her brow furrowed, and she looked around expecting…something.

"Everything okay?" Tristan asked.

"As okay as it's going to get," she said then we followed her inside.

The curtains on the sliding glass doors were still open.

The undead woman sat on the back porch step, looking off into the distance.

Tristan looked at me.

"You ready?" I whispered to Amelia.

Her eyes were wet with unshed tears, but she nodded.

"Mom?" Amelia called, knocking lightly on the glass. "Mom?"

The undead woman didn't move.

Amelia looked at me.

"Caroline?" I whispered with my mind.

"Go away."

"Amelia is here."

"Go away."

"Mom?" Amelia called again then looked at me. "Can you hear her?"

I nodded. "She can hear you."

"What is she saying?" Amelia asked.

I frowned. I didn't want to tell her.

"Caroline, we need your help. There was a scientist…we found a cure. At least, we think so," I said aloud. "We need your help."

"Mom, we think we have a cure for people like you."

"Go away."

"Caroline, you are not like the others. There are more like you who still think, who still exist. We came here—" I began but then she jumped up and came to stand face to face with me.

"I'm not what I was," she said, interrupting me. *"The pain. The hunger. I'm dangerous. Get my daughter out of here."*

"Layla?" Tristan whispered.

I motioned for him to be silent.

"Won't you try? For her sake? What else is left but hope?"

"Mom, Miss Beatrice studied the scientist's notes. There

was something wrong with the flu shot. If you let us, we can try to cure you, to bring you back," Amelia pleaded. "You were a nurse. Please. If you won't do it for yourself, maybe we can save others, but only if we know if it works. Layla said there are others like you, others who didn't lose themselves entirely. Won't you try? If not for you, for them?"

Finally, she relented, her moon-white eyes flashing toward her daughter as her shoulders slumped in defeat.

"We'll come outside," Tristan told her. "We," he said, motioning to Will and Kellimore, "we must restrain you. Beatrice will give the injection."

The undead woman looked up at me. *"My bag. Tell Amelia to bring my bag. My stethoscope."*

"She wants you to get her bag, her stethoscope."

Amelia rushed toward the back of the house.

"Does your heart still beat?" I asked.

"Slowly. Like hypothermia."

"How have you survived? Off the living?" I asked, not wanting the others to hear my question or her answer.

"Animals. This body needs little. But I am a killer, and I still crave," she said, motioning to the rumbled heap of a decayed body lying at the back of the lawn.

"Another like you told me the hunger is uncontrollable at first."

"Yes," she said, her voice thick with sadness.

"Here," Amelia said, reemerging with the bag. The girl looked hopeful.

It felt dangerous to hope.

"We'll come out now," Tristan said, opening the door.

The undead woman stepped away and sat in one of the wooden porch chairs.

I pulled my blade and headed outside.

It was strange to be so close to her. To find her so still.

Tristan pulled off his backpack and took out some rope from inside. "We need to bind your arms, tie them to the chair."

"Palms up," Beatrice told him.

"Sorry, Amelia." Kellimore said. "We should gag her. Beatrice will be very close."

Everyone looked at me.

"It's all right," the woman whispered then closed her eyes.

I nodded to Kellimore. Moving carefully, Will and Tristan quickly bound the woman's arms to the chair while Kellimore secured a gag around her mouth.

"Mom," Amelia whispered. "Mom, I can see your colors. Just a little. I see just flecks. It's going to work. Please, just hold on."

"The stethoscope?" Beatrice asked Amelia.

She nodded, handing it to her.

Moving gingerly, her hands shaking, Beatrice set the stethoscope on the woman's chest. We all paused as she listened.

"Tell her to move it lower," the voice came inside my head.

"Move it lower," I told Beatrice. "As she suggests," I said, motioning to the woman.

"So strange," Beatrice whispered after a moment. "Her heart is beating so slowly. Her respiration is low."

I closed my eyes. *Oh, Jamie, please hold on.*

Digging in the bag once more, Amelia pulled out some alcohol prep wipes and handed them to Beatrice who then cleaned the woman's arm.

The woman's pallor was ashen, her skin pale and blue. It was just like she said, like she'd fallen into an icy pond and just stopped in that state like hypothermia.

"I'm going to do the injection now," Beatrice said, prepping the needle.

Kellimore pulled his gun and aimed it toward Caroline.

"Okay," Beatrice said, then stuck the needle in her arm.

No one breathed.

The undead woman sat perfectly still, but she opened her eyes and watched Beatrice work.

A moment later, Beatrice pulled the syringe away.

Then, we waited.

"Mom?" Amelia whispered.

The woman sat very still.

"Caroline?" I whispered.

"Itching. Hot. My skin is burning," she whispered.

"She feels it. It's itching and burning," I told the others.

"My heart," the undead woman said then. *"Something's wrong."*

"The stethoscope. Quickly," I told Beatrice.

She quickly placed the instrument on the woman's chest. "Her heartbeat is accelerating rapidly. Not good. Not good."

"Her aura is going wild," Amelia said. "Mom. Mom?"

The woman started convulsing then, shaking from side to side.

"Layla? What's she saying?" Tristan asked.

"Nothing." Moving quickly, I removed the gag before she choked on the froth bubbling from her mouth.

"Mom!" Amelia said, reaching out tepidly, but drawing her hand back.

We all stood, staring aghast as Caroline shook.

After a moment, the seizure subsided and the woman's head hung slack.

"Is she gone? Is she dead?" Amelia asked.

I ignored the irony of the question and gently probed. *"Caroline? Caroline?"*

At that, the woman's head snapped up, and she went wild, howling, hissing, and biting at us. Her eyes had turned a terrible red color. The veins on her arms and throat bulged turning dark blue as she struggled against the restraints, snapping at us.

"No, oh no," Amelia said, turning away.

Will grabbed Amelia whose knees went soft, holding her upright.

"It didn't work," Beatrice whispered.

"Caroline," I called to her. *"Caroline, answer me."*

There was no reply.

Spit hung in long strings from her open mouth. She hissed and snapped at us.

"Caroline? Say something."

Nothing.

I shook my head. "She's not answering me."

Amelia cried.

"Let's go inside," Will whispered, leading her away.

"Caroline, please. Can you hear me? Please. For Amelia, please answer me."

Beatrice walked back into the house, Tristan following behind her.

"Look at her," Kellimore said then. "She looks different. Not like the zombies, but not like she was either. Look at her eyes."

He was right. The white of her eyes was gone. They were bloody red, but I could see the blue of her iris at the center.

"I don't understand," I whispered.

"Doctor Gustav was wrong, that's all," Kellimore said. "This wasn't the cure. But we won't give up. We can find a way," he said reassuringly, but his words felt empty.

The truth was, if we could not cure the undead, then we could not save ourselves from the disease. We would have to rely on the protection of the seelie and their enchantments. It was the only way left to survive.

CHAPTER TWENTY-EIGHT

CRICKET

"NOT GOOD," LOGAN SAID as we approached the small hometown medical center.

Chase slowed the Jeep. At the medical center, every door was open, every window broken, and the number of undead milling around was…well, more than I wanted to count.

"Yeah, that's a lot of zombies," Zoey said.

"Too many," Chase agreed.

"Still, we need those supplies," Logan added

Zoey snapped her fingers. "Doc Dickerson. Veterinarian. He'd have a lot of needles and stuff. Probably no one thought of that place…in time. Turn there," she said, pointing.

Logan looked out the back. "We've got some trailers."

I frowned. "And I'm sure a lot more coming. They follow noise."

"We'll need to be quick then. We aren't that far from the vet's," Zoey said. "Turn right here," she said, guiding Chase onto a side street. "There."

The place looked clear, at least for the moment. We ran to the door and looked inside.

I tried the door. "Locked," I said. With a heave, I smashed out the glass.

Clicking on the flashlight, Zoey led us inside.

The place was dark and there was a scent of decay in the

air. The small waiting room had dusty red chairs and images of puppies and kittens on the walls.

Zoey headed behind the reception counter. "Looking for keys," she said, opening drawers as the rest of us scanned around. She shook her head. "Nothing."

"This way," Chase said, and we headed down the hallway.

Luckily, the exam rooms were open. In the first one, Zoey filled her bag with everything she could find in the cupboards. Chase stopped in the next room.

I motioned for Logan to follow me.

When we came to the next room, we found it locked.

"Must be the medicines," Logan said, trying the door.

I nodded then looked over the lock. "Got a knife?" I asked him.

He pulled a hunting knife from his belt and handed it to me. Wiggling the blade inside the door jam, I worked the lock. With one final twist, the lock popped. "There we go," I said then pushed open the door. I flashed my light around. We were in the right place. The shelves were lined with box after box of medical supplies: syringes, vials, pills, bandages, and equipment.

"Here," I called to the others. "We hit the mother lode."

"There we go," Chase said as he joined us. He eyed the shelves. Scouting around, he found a cooler and started filling it up.

"I'll sweep the rest of the place," I said then headed back out.

I found the break room just down the hall. Not much there but an old strawberry Pop-Tart. It was a month over its best-by date, but I wasn't even sorry. Ripping open that aluminum packet, I munched as I walked. Funny how the smell of death didn't even bother me much anymore. Used to be anything that smelled too tangy would set my stomach on edge. Guess I'd gotten used to it.

When I got to the back of the building, I found the sad source of the awful smell. Inside the kennels were the decayed remains of too many dogs. My heart hurt. It made me so sad to think they'd starved to death locked up like that.

"We've got it all," Chase called.

I turned to go back when I heard a thump outside. Great. Had the first of the undead gotten there already?

I went to the back door to see that it led into an outside kennel area. The scene was a lot like the image inside.

Something bumped the door once more.

Standing up on my tiptoes, I pressed my forehead against the glass and looked down. To my surprise, two little brown eyes were looking up at me.

I opened the door slowly. When I did, I found a small, very thin dog sitting on the other side of the door.

"Well, I'll be. Look at you," I said, then bent down on one knee to pat him. Poor little thing was nothing more than skin and bones. He licked my face, pawing at my knee. "How in the world did you make it?" I asked then stepped into the small space.

All the kennels were closed. One kennel, however, had a hole in the fence. In the back of the dog run was a storage shed. From the looks of it, the little dog had chewed his way through the door.

"Poor little guy," I said, bending to pet him once more. He was a cute little thing, brown eyes, pink nose, and white blaze on his chest. Maybe some kind of dachshund and beagle mix. I looked at his collar. "Frankie," I said, reading the name.

He yipped once, tail wagging happily. "Well, Frankie. You just restored my faith in the world. Now let me restore yours because I'm pretty sure I saw some dog treats inside," I said then turned and headed back, my new friend following along behind me.

When I turned the corner, I found the others waiting for me.

"Look what I found," I said with a smile.

Chase grinned. "You *sure* you know what you found? Last time you had a dog…"

"Logan?"

Logan laughed. "No. He's just a dog."

"All right then, your clearance is approved," I told Frankie as we headed back toward the front. I grabbed the plastic jar of dog biscuits off the counter, tossing several to Frankie, and we went outside. We were just in time because the horde of zombies from the medical center had just found us.

"Crap. Everyone in," Zoey said, slipping into the driver's seat.

"Man, they had some hustle in their step," Chase said.

"Well, we damned near rang the supper bell for them," I replied, setting the apprehensive dog inside. Once he saw the biscuits, though, he warmed up to the idea.

"Okay. Change of direction," Zoey said then pulled the Jeep onto the grass. We bumped across two back lawns and then crossed a small park, dodging picnic pavilions and two of the wandering undead. Then she pulled the Jeep back onto the road. Turning, she headed back across town. When she made one last turn, however, we found ourselves at a barricaded intersection. On the other side, a lot of undead were trying to push through.

"Well, that's new," she said, putting the Jeep into reverse.

"Across the courthouse parking lot," Logan suggested as he eyed a group of undead moving toward us.

"Why are there so many of them floating around?" I asked as I gazed out the window. My nerves were on edge. I knew this wasn't good.

"Something must have attracted them. We just got in the mix," Chase said.

And then we heard it. Gunfire.

"Shit," Zoey said, then turned the Jeep down a side street and around a colossal old building then into a parking lot where we came across an unexpected scene. In the center of the parking lot, a guy and a girl were standing on the roof of a tractor trailer shooting at a horde that had collected around them.

My eyes took in the scene real quick. Between the roof of the tractor trailer and the building had been some sort of makeshift bridge which was now hanging, broken, from a window in an upper floor of the courthouse.

"Look," I said, pointing. "They must have got stuck up there."

"Are you seeing what I'm seeing?" Zoey said to Logan.

"Yes," Logan replied.

"What do we do?" Zoey asked.

"What we always do," I replied, casting a glance at Chase. "We save the living." I reached into the back and pulled out the best find recovered from Moonshine Pete's house, an automatic weapon. I handed it to Chase.

"We're going to draw every asshole in town," he warned.

"Doesn't matter. Let's finish these, grab those two kids, and get the hell out of here."

"Better get down," I told Frankie who whimpered and laid on the floor.

A moment later, the automatic started rattling.

The two kids on the roof looked in our direction in shock.

I jumped out and started picking off the undead coming from behind. Logan joined me. As soon as we had cleared a path, I waved toward the guy and girl. "Come on," I called to them.

The two paused and looked at us, unsure what to do.

"Brian! Brianna! Here," Zoey yelled to them.

Okay, not strangers. Well, that explained the comment.

The pair scurried down the ladder on the back of the semi and rushed toward us. Zoey and Chase picked off the advancing horde while Logan and I took care of those coming around the back. But they kept coming.

"Getting swamped," I called.

"Here too," Chase yelled, and then I heard it…well, I heard nothing. "I'm out of ammo."

"Zoey?" the boy called.

"Get in, get in," she told him. I turned to see that the horde had made their way to us, Zoey now fighting them hand-to-hand.

I pulled my machete and ran back.

"Logan, Chase, get in," I called. "Everyone, let's go."

I saw Zoey swing her baseball bat hard, knocking the undead away so the pair that had been on the truck could get into the Jeep. Chase slid into the driver's seat as Logan made a dash for the vehicle, the newcomers following behind.

"Zoey, come on," I called to her.

"Brian and Brianna first. Get in. I'm not leaving you again," she called, holding off the undead so the pair could get past.

I rushed to her aid as Chase turned on the engine. I cast a glance back.

"They're in. They're in," I told Zoey.

Zoey and I ran back to the Jeep.

"Go on," I told Zoey.

Turning, I shot an undead man advancing fast toward me, the others following hard behind him.

"Cricket, let's go," Chase yelled.

Then, I saw it. It was like everything around me slowed. An undead man, moving quickly, blasted out from behind the dumpster nearby and grabbed for Zoey. She was too close. Too close.

"No," I screamed, pushing Zoey out of the way.

Then, I felt it.

It was like a thousand wasps bit my arm all at once.

"Cricket," Zoey yelled, pulling me back. She grabbed my machete and sliced the man's head off.

His teeth released.

His head fell to the ground.

I could feel arms on me as others pulled me into the Jeep. The vehicle shot off, away from the terrible scene.

Pain shot up my arm to my shoulder. Nausea swept over me.

"Cricket! What the hell happened?" Chase called.

"She pushed me out of the way," Zoey said.

It all happened so fast.

So fast.

My arm felt like it was on fire.

"Cricket, are you all right? Zoey, what's going on? Cricket?" Chase called.

"She's bit," Zoey said.

I looked up at Zoey who was holding me against her chest while Logan worked quickly to tourniquet my arm.

"Cricket," Zoey said softly.

"It's okay. Gotta save the living," I whispered then closed my eyes.

CHAPTER TWENTY-NINE

AMELIA

I STUCK MY HAND OUT THE WINDOW, feeling the warm breeze. I closed my eyes and let the air brush my face.

"Goddess Mother, thank you for the chance to speak to my mother one last time. It is a rare and sacred blessing. Thank you for that."

We'd stayed awhile after the injection in hope there would be some sort of change, but there wasn't. Layla wasn't able to reach my mother again.

No one spoke as we drove home. The cure had failed. No matter how the doctor's tests had turned out in her animal trials, it had failed in a human trial. I was so sure it would work. I had seen my mother's light, just small flecks of it fighting all around her. Now, her color had just imploded, everything turning black and red. It had been too much to look at.

Layla, who sat between me and Tristan, held my hand. The energy coming off her, warm and sympathetic, comforted me. I knew what the failure meant to Layla. There was no hope for her fiancé now either. The idea made me terribly sad.

When we arrived at the gates of Witch Wood, Tristan opened the truck door and moved to get out.

"No," I said. "Let me practice."

"All right, Amelia."

I slid out and stood in front of the gate.

There was no cure.

There was no hope.

But maybe just a little bit of magic could still save us.

CHAPTER THIRTY
CRICKET

I OPENED MY EYES JUST A CRACK. Chase and Logan were laying me down in the billiard room.

"What the hell? What happened?" Ariel said.

"Where's Vella?" Chase asked.

"Upstairs."

"Get her. Now. You, go find Madame Knightly," Chase said, but he sounded real far away, and my ears had started ringing real bad.

Footsteps rushed away.

I coughed hard and felt the tang of blood on my lips.

"Dammit. God dammit," Chase said, tearing a strip of his shirt to wipe the blood away.

"Don't take the lord's name in vain," I whispered.

Chase laughed.

"Tristan?" I asked.

"Still gone."

"Bar the doors. If she turns, we cannot let her out," I heard Madame Knightly say followed by the sound of doors clattering shut.

"No. No fucking way. We need that medicine. She's still here. We need that cure right now. Where's Beatrice?" Chase said.

"Still gone," someone said.

"Mommy, what's happening?" I heard one of the girls ask.

"Zoey, go get that shot. Logan, go with her and get the right one," Chase said.

A flood of feet ran the other direction.

"We don't know if it works. They aren't back yet." Was it Jamie who said that? No, couldn't have been. Jamie was dead.

My body jerked. Someone poured cold water over my arm.

"Cricket," I heard Vella exclaim followed by the sound of small bells as she rushed across the room. "What happened?"

"Bit," Chase replied.

"Maybe if we take her arm it will stop the infection," someone said. Was it Darius?

"No," I heard Logan call. "No, I've got it. I…I don't know how to give a shot."

There was silence for a moment. My head was ringing like a bell. Everyone and everything felt really far away. I felt like I was going to be sick.

"I can do it," I heard Frenchie say. "I studied phlebotomy for a semester. I can do it."

A moment later, I saw a mountain of red hair in front of me.

"Mommy?"

"Stay there, girls."

"Oh look, a puppy!" one of the girls squeaked.

"Cricket," I heard Frenchie say softly. "Cricket? Can you hear me? I'm going to inject you now." Someone held my arm tightly. I felt a sharp poke.

I closed my eyes. My head felt so heavy. I felt hot tears slide down the side of my face.

"Don't leave me," Vella whispered in my ear.

I opened my mouth to speak, but my words failed me.

And then there was nothing but darkness.

CHAPTER THIRTY-ONE

LAYLA

WHEN THE TRUCK PULLED TO A STOP behind an unfamiliar Jeep in the driveway outside Witch Wood, a terrible feeling swept over me.

"Something's wrong," I whispered.

Amelia nodded. "I feel it too."

Vella rushed out, Madame Knightly appearing at the door behind her.

"Tristan," Vella called.

"Vella? What is it?" he asked.

Vella's face was deathly pale. "There was a problem."

Tristan looked from Vella to Madame Knightly. "Where's Cricket?"

Vella looked scared. "Tristan…Cricket's group got pinned down. She was bit, but we gave her the antidote the doctor—"

"What? No," Beatrice said, rushing inside, all of us following along behind her.

"Where is she?" Amelia asked, panic filling her voice.

"In the gentlemen's parlor," Madame Knightly replied.

We raced to the room to find Cricket lying on the billiard table. Frenchie was inspecting a bandage on her arm and checking her for fever. My stomach knotted at the sight. Oh no, not her.

"What is it?" Madame Knightly asked as she followed

along behind us.

"The cure," I replied. "It didn't work."

She look confused. "Are you certain?"

"Amelia's mother…it sent her into a kind of frenzy. After that, she was gone," I explained.

"Cricket," Tristan said with a gasp, taking her hand. "She's cold."

Beatrice took Cricket's hand and felt her pulse.

"Well?" Vella asked.

"Sounds okay," Beatrice said. "Steady."

"What happened?" I asked Chase.

"We found two kids. Zoey knew them. We saved them from a horde. Cricket held the line, made sure Zoey got into the vehicle. She…she was protecting the others."

"Zoey okay?" I asked.

Chase nodded.

"Had she turned?" Beatrice asked.

"No."

"I need the medical bag from the library," Beatrice said.

"I'll get it," Logan said.

"Who were the two kids you found?" Amelia asked.

"Um, Brian, maybe. And a girl. Something with a B," Chase replied.

"Brianna?"

"Yeah, that was it."

"Cricket?" Tristan whispered, holding her hand in his. "Do you hear me?" Tears streamed down his face.

"How long? How long ago did you give her the shot?" Beatrice asked as she continued to examine Cricket.

"About thirty minutes," Frenchie said. "I bandaged the wound."

"Let's have a look," Beatrice answered.

Frenchie began to slowly unwind the bandage as Amelia looked closely at Cricket.

"Cricket?" Tristan whispered, reaching out to touch her face.

My heart nearly broke at the sight.

"Bad. I need to get her going with some antibiotics. The wound looks clean. You did well," Beatrice told Frenchie.

My eyes, however, were on Amelia who was rubbing her hands together very slowly.

"Amelia?" Madame Knightly said. Her inquiry caught all our attention. Even Tristan looked up at the girl.

"She's there," Amelia said. "I see her. She's fighting. Her aura is so strong. Hot pink and yellow," Amelia said with a smile. "The darkness that surrounds the wound is fighting her," she said then turned to Tristan and the others. "Please, everyone, can you give me some space?"

We all stepped back and watched.

Amelia took a deep breath, focusing as she began moving slowly around Cricket's body. Her hands worked as if she was pulling something off of Cricket.

"See. See everything," my grandmother had told me. I tried to focus, tried to see what Amelia could see. But I couldn't. I cast a glance at Vella. I knew that she, like me, had eyes into the otherworld. But whatever it was that Amelia could see, I could tell by the expression on Vella's face, she couldn't see it either.

Amelia worked slowly. "It's coming off," Amelia whispered as she continued to circle Cricket's body.

I closed my eyes. *"Cricket?"* I whispered with my mind.

But there was nothing, no answer.

And I was glad.

When Amelia got to the wound, she labored hard. Her breathing accelerated. Sweat dripped down Amelia's forehead, and she turned very pale.

"That's my good girl," Madame Knightly whispered under her breath.

Struggling, Amelia finally tugged at…something. She pulled and pulled, grunting and straining, then finally whatever it was seemed to snap. Amelia lost her balance and tumbled backward a few steps.

Taking a huge gasp of air, Cricket sat up, her eyes wide open and bright blue.

"Tristan?" she called then slumped back.

Tristan rushed to her side.

"I'm here, my lovely tilt girl."

"I found a dog," Cricket whispered, making everyone smile.

Beatrice checked Cricket's pulse. After a few minutes, she nodded. "She's okay."

Tristan wept, his sense of relief palpable.

I felt like I finally exhaled.

I crossed the room to Amelia who looked like she was about to drop. I put my arm around her waist and led her toward the kitchen. "You need to drink something," I told her.

"Yeah," she said, nodding absently.

In the kitchen, two strangers sat at the breakfast nook, both of them eating heaping plates of food. They looked up when we entered.

"Amelia?" the girl said in surprise.

"Brianna? Brian?" Amelia said, shaking her head with confusion. The girl's knees went soft. I barely kept her upright.

The boy she'd called Brian crossed the room, helping me get Amelia into a chair at the table.

"I…I don't understand. How…" Amelia said.

"After we lost you, we didn't know what to do. We went

back into town. We've been living in the attic of the courthouse all winter. Brighton is a mess, but lately the zombies have been getting really bad. More and more of them showing up. We got stuck just when Zoey and the others showed up today. They saved us," Brian said.

"That girl out there," Brianna said, looking toward the front of the house. "She got bit. They gave her some sort of shot. Is it working?"

"It looks like it. I'm Layla, by the way," I said.

"Brianna, and my brother, Brian," the girl introduced.

"We were together at the beginning," Amelia said. "We got separated in the mist."

"I'm sorry, Amelia," Brian said. "We tried to find you. We just...we couldn't find Witch Wood again."

Amelia nodded.

I rummaged through the cupboards until I found honey which I mixed into a glass of water, sweetening it as much as I could.

"Here," I said, handing it to Amelia. "You need sugar. My grandmother was a medium. She always had to drink something sweet after a session. She used to say it drained the sugar from her."

"Thank you," Amelia said absently, drinking the honey water. She seemed really out of it, the episode exhausting her.

"What...what's going on?" Brianna asked then. "Amelia? Are you okay?"

"I had to help Cricket. Layla, I feel really tired."

I nodded. "Drink. I'll get Chase, and we'll take you to your room. You need to get some rest," I said then headed back to the gentlemen's parlor. Amelia was just a wisp of a thing. Surely Chase could carry her upstairs.

When I returned, I saw Beatrice checking Cricket's vitals.

Tristan and Vella sat nearby as Chase, Darius, and Madame Knightly watched on.

I realized then that Chase was totally focused on Cricket. Through the window, however, I spotted Kellimore out in the driveway standing in front of the truck, the hood open.

I cast a glance at Cricket, whose color had returned to her cheeks, then headed outside.

"Hey," I called to Kellimore. "I need your muscles."

Kellimore looked around the hood of the truck at me and raised an eyebrow.

The expression made me smile despite myself.

"Amelia. Can you carry her upstairs? She's not feeling well."

"Sure," he said, dropping the hood. "Cricket…is she…" he said, shaking his head. "Spent all winter bickering with her. She's a master at it. I'd hate for—"

"She seems like she's going to be okay."

"Then the antidote does work?"

"I'm not sure. I mean, it looks like maybe, if the person doesn't actually…"

"You mean, if they don't die first," Kellimore said.

"That would explain why it didn't work on Amelia's mom."

"Yeah," Kellimore said then frowned. "That was awful."

I nodded.

In the kitchen, Amelia sat looking into her glass, her eyes watery. Brianna was holding her hand.

"Amelia?" I called gently.

"Yeah?" she asked absently.

"Kellimore will help you upstairs."

"Okay," she whispered.

With that, I helped Amelia stand, and we walked slowly to the steps.

"Cricket?" she asked then, looking back toward the parlor.

"She's doing okay now. I think you saved her."

Amelia smiled.

I motioned to Kellimore who gently lifted her.

"Don't tell me you have a room on the sixth floor," Kellimore said.

"Second floor. By the stairs. Where's Logan?"

"In the library helping Beatrice."

Moving ahead, I went to Amelia's room and opened the door. Kellimore lowered her into the bed. I pulled her shoes off.

"Layla, can you find Zoey?" she asked.

I nodded. "Need anything else?"

She shook her head.

"I'll come back and check on you," I told her.

"Thank you."

With that, I nodded to Kellimore, and we headed back into the hallway.

"I'm going to find Zoey. Thanks for helping."

"Sure. You're welcome to my muscles any time," Kellimore said.

"I'll keep that in mind," I said with a smile then went upstairs to Zoey's room.

"Hey, Layla?" Kellimore called.

I stopped at the top of the third floor landing and looked back down at him. "Yeah?"

"Can you read everyone's mind?"

I smiled. "No. I'm a medium. I can only hear the dead. Why?"

Kellimore smiled. "No reason."

"Thanks again."

"Sure. Always happy to help you," he said then turned and

headed back down stairs.

I stood and watched him go. I hadn't even realized I was doing so until Ariel appeared on the stairs in front of me.

"How is Cricket?" she asked. I realized then that Ariel looked pale. Was she sick?

"She's doing okay."

Ariel smiled then followed my gaze.

"He *is* cute," she said then smiled at me. "Well, I'm going to check on Cricket. And I'm going to see if they have anything to eat with banana in it. All day long I was craving dried banana chips. Weird. I don't even like bananas," she said then headed downstairs.

Blushing, I turned and went in search of Zoey.

CHAPTER THIRTY-TWO

LAYLA

ONCE CRICKET WAS STABILIZED, they moved her into the library where Logan and the others had set up a makeshift medical station. At Madame Knightly's suggestion, someone had to stand guard just in case.

It was just coming to the close of my shift on watch, sometime around midnight, when Cricket opened her eyes.

Tristan was asleep in a chair nearby, and I'd sent Vella upstairs to rest about an hour before.

Keeping me company, however, was the tiny brown dog Zoey told me Cricket had saved.

"Tristan?" Cricket called softly.

"He's asleep," I said, setting my sword aside. I rose and stood beside her. "How are you feeling?"

"Like someone hit me on the side of the head with a shovel."

"I bet."

"Everything's real hazy," she said, looking down at her arm. "What happened, exactly?"

"You were bit," I replied. "At least, that's what they told me."

"Bit," she said, then looked down at her arm. "I remember. So why am I still alive?"

"Doctor Gustav's injection."

"Then it worked. What about Amelia's mother?"

"No good."

"Oh," Cricket said softly.

"Amelia helped you come back."

"*The High Priestess*," Cricket said absently.

"Sorry?"

"Just something from Vella's tarot. *The High Priestess* will stand between the worlds using her magic," Cricket said sleepily.

I nodded as I thought on her words. "Oh," I said, reaching down to pick up the nervous bundle of canine. "Here's someone who's been worried about you."

Cricket cracked her eyes open. "Hey, Frankie."

The little dog wagged his tail.

"Frenchie's girls gave him a bath. And his stomach is full."

Cricket smiled. "Little guy," she said, reaching out to pat his head with her good arm. She looked up at me. "Layla, I think we're going to make it out of this. I had a dream. It was real fuzzy, but I saw this place, a little town sitting beside a lake. We were all there, even some new people. It was a good place. And we were safe. There was a river too. And I saw you at this small little cabin in the woods. Layla, we're going to make it."

"I hope so," I told her. "But for now, you need to rest. You're making history. First woman to survive a zombie bite."

"I guess so. New history now, right?"

"All new."

"You're the historian. You taking notes?"

I smiled at her. "Sure."

The little dog curled up at Cricket's feet. He sighed contentedly.

"Get some sleep. Will is coming in soon. And Tristan is here."

"Thanks, Layla," Cricket whispered.

"Get some rest."

She smiled then drifted back to sleep.

I glanced over at Tristan. He was sitting in the most awkward position, his neck at a weird angle, but he was at her side. His dedication moved me, and made a lump of guilt gnaw at my stomach.

Okay, so if Jamie wasn't at Claddagh-Basel, where was he? And if the cure didn't work on those who'd already turned, did it even matter?

Maybe it was time to just accept he was gone.

But if I did, wasn't that giving up?

"Layla?" Will whispered.

I smiled at him. "She just woke up, spoke a little. She's okay. She's normal."

"Well," Will said with a sigh. "At least we know it works if you get it before you turn. Sad about Amelia's mom. About broke my heart."

"Mine too."

"All right. I've got the watch now," he said then looked down at Cricket. "A shame," he added, smiling down on her.

"What is?"

"That she's taken. She's beautiful."

I chuckled.

"'Night, Will."

"'Night, Layla."

I went upstairs, stopping to make a few checks.

Elle had been sleeping most of the day. I slipped into her room, stopping to check her for fever. Thankfully, she was all right. She didn't even stir, just kept on snoring loudly. I passed Frenchie's room. There I found her, Kira, and Susan snuggled up tight next to one another.

Sighing, I headed to my own room. Pulling off my boots

and setting my shashka aside, I sat down at the side of the bed and pulled out my engagement ring, looking at it under the light of the full moon. I set it on my bedside table and laid down, looking at the ring. Jamie and I had been stupid to think that there was any future in front of us. The world didn't work like that anymore.

But then I remembered Cricket's dream.

In her dream, she'd seen Hamletville.

CHAPTER THIRTY-THREE

LAYLA

IT MUST HAVE BEEN JUST BEFORE DAWN when someone shook my shoulder very lightly.

"Layla?" someone whispered. "Layla?"

I sat up and reached for my shashka before I even opened my eyes only to find Amelia standing at my bedside.

"Amelia? Everything okay?"

"Don't get up," she said then sat down at the side of my bed. "Thank you for earlier. Your grandmother was a medium?"

"Yes," I said groggily, pulling myself up. "I inherited the gift from her."

"Layla, I want to go check on my mother. I want to see if there is any change. What I did for Cricket was hard. I never did anything so hard in my life. My powers seem to be…growing. You saw what happened that day outside the store."

"Well, yes and no. It was like…well, like magic."

"Zoey says that maybe I'm a Jedi." She smiled then sighed. "I want to try one more time. I…I can't stand the thought of leaving my mother like that. She was a good person. Maybe the medicine didn't work, but maybe I can try like I did with Cricket."

"What did Madame Knightly say?"

"I…I didn't tell her."

"Logan?"

"Him either. After what happened yesterday, it feels foolish to go back out. Brian and Brianna said there are so many more zombies. But I need to try. Just once more. I was hoping you'd help me."

"I'll take you. We'll go quick and quiet. Sun is almost up."

Amelia smiled. "I'll let you get ready. Meet you outside?"

"Don't suppose there is a back way we can slip out?"

"Not unless you're a cat."

"I guess that's a no."

Amelia nodded, rose, and then left.

Maybe it was a fool's errand, maybe it was putting ourselves in harm's way for nothing, but the truth was, I wanted to try again as much as she did. I'd give it one last chance. For Jamie.

CHAPTER THIRTY-FOUR

LAYLA

WHEN I GOT DOWNSTAIRS, I wasn't surprised to see that Zoey was waiting along with Amelia.

"Can't shake me," Zoey said. "I got up to see if Amelia was feeling okay, and I found her dressed. So..."

I nodded. "It's okay. More guns are always good."

"Don't know how much help I am. I screwed up like some stupid bimbo in a horror movie yesterday and nearly got Cricket killed."

"Nearly, but not," Amelia said. "Ready?"

I nodded.

"Need to push the truck to the gate if we want to get out of here with any subterfuge," Zoey said then slipped into the driver's seat and put the truck into neutral. Amelia and I pushed as Zoey steered the truck down the driveway to the gate. Good thing it was a downhill slope.

Once Amelia got the gate opened, Zoey started the vehicle. Amelia closed the gate, casting the enchantment on the property once more, then we both climbed in. Once more, the mist seemed to envelope the place.

"I'm never going to get used to that," Zoey said.

Amelia nodded but didn't say anything.

Zoey guided the truck down the misty road toward town. The early morning air was cool and smelled of the woods. I could just catch the scents of pine and new ferns.

We drove quietly into town, taking the turns slowly, watching for the undead.

"It's quiet," Amelia said.

"If I say 'it's too quiet' then all hell will break loose. It's a given. So, let me just say 'yep'," Zoey replied.

I frowned as I looked out the window. Brighton had a lot of meandering undead. So, where were they now? Too quiet indeed.

"Did you talk to B and B?" Zoey asked.

"Just a little. I was kinda out of it," Amelia said.

"I talked to them last night after you went to sleep."

"Are they…are they angry at us?" Amelia asked, her voice quivering.

"No. They were feeling guilty too, thought they lost us in the woods. I had to try to explain what was going on at Witch Wood. They were…unconvinced."

"I'm so glad they made it. It's lucky you were there."

"You? Believe in dumb luck?"

Amelia smiled.

"They had it hard," Zoey said. "Did you notice? They were so thin."

"Yeah," Amelia said with a sigh.

As I listened to their conversation, I looked out the window. The sense of responsibility and guilt in their voices echoed the feelings in my heart. Keeping people alive wasn't easy. At least now, with a cure, we might be able to survive.

Zoey pulled the truck into Amelia's driveway.

We sat there for a moment.

"It might not be any better," I warned Amelia.

"I know," she said.

"And possibly worse."

"I just have to see one last time. Then, I can let it go."

I nodded, squeezed her hand, and then we slid out of the truck.

Zoey was carrying a pistol in one hand and a baseball bat in the other. I pulled my blade, and we headed toward the house.

Amelia gently laid her hand on the oak tree then we headed inside.

When we got to the porch, I smelled an odd scent lingering in the air.

"Is that cigarette smoke?" Zoey whispered.

"Stay back," I told the girls.

Zoey held the screen door while I slowly opened the door. The scent of cigarette smoke wafted from the house. I looked back at Amelia who looked like she wanted to spring past me, but I shook my head.

I stepped in slowly. The house was dark. The sliding glass door to the back was open. Moving carefully, trying to not make any sound as I crossed the floor, I approached the back patio. All my senses were on edge.

"Come," a raspy voice called in my mind.

"Caroline?"

"Come."

Moving carefully, I stepped outside. She was still sitting in the chair where we'd left her yesterday, but her restraints were undone. She held a cigarette. A long ash hung on it, the ember burning between her fingers, but she didn't seem to feel it.

"Caroline?"

She looked up at me.

I gasped. Her face was still pale but now mottled by dark veins. Her eyes were completely bloodshot save the small blue irises.

"Can you hear me?"

"Yes."

"Can you speak?"

"No."

"Layla?" Amelia called.

"No. Don't let her see."

"Let her come. She can help you. Maybe she can heal you."

"No."

Before I could intervene either way, Zoey and Amelia appeared behind me.

"Mom?" Amelia whispered.

"Stay back."

"She says to stay back."

"Mom?" Amelia said, looking closely at her mother.

"She can't speak," I told them. "What do you see, Amelia?"

Amelia shook her head. "Nothing. I don't see anything."

"What do you mean?" Zoey asked.

"There's just…nothing."

"Caroline? How are you? Can you tell me? How are you?"

"Not dead. Not alive. Not like before," she said, staring off into the distance.

"Do you have a heartbeat?" I asked.

"Not that I can feel."

"Breath?"

She looked at the cigarette. *"No."*

I shook my head.

Amelia sat down in a chair nearby just staring at her mother.

"There is no time. Everything just blurs. I'm trapped inside a corpse. Please shoot me."

"How can I do that with Amelia here?"

"Mercy. Please give me mercy. It didn't work. I am nothing. No one.

I am a ghost inside a carcass. End it."

I looked at Amelia.

"What is it? What did she say?"

"She asked for mercy."

Amelia stared at her mother. "Mom?"

The woman turned and looked at her.

Amelia gasped.

"The injection made it worse," Zoey said.

I nodded.

"Tell Amelia to say goodbye. Her mother is gone. Please give me mercy."

"Amelia…"

"I know," Amelia whispered.

"What should we do?" Zoey asked.

Amelia moved toward her mother.

"Tell her not to get close. I cannot control myself."

"Don't get close."

Amelia stopped.

"We'll give her mercy," I said then reached to take Zoey's gun.

"Layla, take Amelia inside," Zoey told me.

I looked her in the eye. She had known this woman. Maybe it was better this way. I nodded to Zoey then moved to lead Amelia away.

"Mom?" Amelia whispered.

"Goodbye, Amelia. I love you."

"She said goodbye and that she loves you."

"Goodbye…I love you too," she said then turned to me and wept as I led her back into the house. I led her into the living room then braced myself, and her, for the sound. It felt like it took an eternity, but in reality, just a moment had passed. The gunshot rang so loudly that both Amelia and I shook.

A moment later, Zoey joined us.

"Amelia," she whispered. "I'm so sorry."

"It's okay. Thank you, Zoey," she said, then we went out onto the front porch.

The moment we stepped outside, however, we all stopped.

Amelia gasped then moved backward.

Now we knew where Brighton's undead were.

They were here.

All of them.

CHAPTER THIRTY-FIVE
LAYLA

"OH MY GOD," ZOEY WHISPERED.

"Back inside, back inside. Now," I yelled, pushing the girls back into the house. I slammed the front door closed behind me, locking it.

"Through the back. Amelia, don't look."

We raced through the back of the house and out onto the back lawn.

Caroline's body lay slumped over in the seat, a ghastly gunshot wound to the back of the head. Amelia shielded her eyes. It was a horrific sight, but there was no time to mourn. We ran toward the back fence. Zoey went over, followed by Amelia, just as the undead crashed through the gate surrounding the property.

"Where did they come from?" Zoey asked as I dropped onto the other side of the fence. We took off in a run.

"Just had to say it was too quiet, didn't you?" I told her as we rushed across the neighbor's lawn and on to the adjoining street. But I knew the truth. I had seen this often enough to know that when the undead showed up en masse, it usually meant the kitsune, and some vampires, were right behind.

"Witch Wood," Amelia said. "We need to get back to Witch Wood."

"This way," Zoey said as we raced down the block, turning

down a side street.

"They're everywhere," Amelia said as we ran.

She was right. Around every corner, every side street, the undead thronged.

The pawns had arrived.

"Here, here," Zoey said as she led us into the parking lot of the Brighton Car Cabana. She ran toward the main building as she fumbled in her pockets.

"Go on," I called to the girls. "I'll hold them off."

They raced ahead as I stopped to take on the undead who were right behind us. My blade moving fast, I swung at an undead man who grabbed at me. His body was so soft that the sword ripped him in two diagonally from the shoulder to the waist. His body slipped sideways, falling with a mushy splash onto the ground. The heap of purplish and reddish brown guts were loaded with maggots. The smell made me gag. I jumped onto the hood of a car, decapitating the undead woman who came near. Pausing for a moment, I scanned the oncoming horde. They were all decayed. There were none of the others among them.

Behind me, an engine roared to life.

"Layla," Amelia yelled.

I looked back to see Zoey and Amelia pull out of the showroom in a classic Mustang, the muscle car's engine rumbling.

Shaking the blood and guts off my blade, I joined them, sliding onto the bucket seat beside Amelia. I slammed the door shut as Zoey gunned the engine.

She raced across town toward the old dirt road leading toward Witch Wood.

"What the actual fuck?" Zoey said. "Where did they all come from?"

"The kitsune. This is the third time I've seen this happen. The undead come first, then the vampires, then the kitsune."

"It's morning, sun is out," Amelia said.

"And the vampires are decimated. The undead will reach Witch Wood," I told them. "The kitsune are leading them."

"But we'll be okay, right?" Zoey asked. "Madame Knightly has enchanted the walls."

"With the same magic the kitsune use," I replied.

"We need to get back, to warn the others. We need to get everyone out of Witch Wood," Amelia said.

"And go where?" Zoey asked.

"Wait," Amelia said, setting her hand on Zoey's arm. "Don't go directly to Witch Wood. Stop there," she said, pointing toward a nearly-hidden road along the way.

"The gorge?"

"We'll hide the car and go by foot. The engine is too loud. We don't want anyone to follow us or..."

"Or hear us coming."

"Shit," Zoey said, turning the car down the grassy road.

Zoey pulled the car into a rocky and overgrown parking lot. An old, broken-down wooden fence lined the edge of a steep cliff. Climbing out of the car, I looked over the ledge. Below was a large pool of water. Even from this angle, I could see bodies lying on the banks below.

"Let's go," Zoey said, pulling her gun.

We ran through the woods toward Witch Wood. Just as we reached the spot in the road near the gate to Witch Wood, Amelia grabbed us both and pulled us down.

From the cover of the dense forest, we stopped and looked.

There we saw something we hadn't expected.

The gate to Witch Wood was perfectly clear.

And it had been smashed off its hinges.

CHAPTER THIRTY-SIX

CRICKET

WHEN I WOKE UP, MY HEAD ACHED and my arm hurt. But I wasn't a zombie.

I sat up slowly, inspecting the bandage on my arm. My skin all around the wound looked okay, painful, but not infected. Amber-colored medicine bottles sat on the table beside me. There were a lot of them. No wonder my head felt woozy.

I smiled to see the little dog I'd found dancing around. I bent to pet him. Yep, definitely woozy.

"What is it, boy? You excited?" I asked him, but as I watched him prance, I realized what the problem was. He needed to go outside. I looked over at Tristan who was still sleeping. Chase was also snoring in a chair nearby.

I had to chuckle. Some guard he was. If I had turned into a zombie, he would have been in trouble. But I was fine. There was no use just lying around.

"Shh," I whispered to the little dog. "Let's go."

Moving slowly, feeling like I'd had one too many Coronas, I made my way to the front of the house. I'd just let the dog out, get some air, and then come back.

The house was real quiet. I gave the door a hard shove then followed the little dog outside. He ran, at once, to pee all over the tires of the Jeep we'd nabbed from the car lot. I was surprised to see, however, that the truck was gone. Who'd gone back out? And especially after yesterday?

I crossed the driveway and leaned against the lamppost while the little dog sniffed all around. When he finished his business, I turned to go back inside. Just then, the dog stopped, his ears and tail poking up on alert.

"What is it?" I asked.

And then I saw it.

At the edge of the field was a glowing ball of blue light.

"I saw you from the upstairs window. What are you doing outside?" Vella asked, coming up from behind me.

"Vella?"

"You should be resting."

"Vella, look," I said, pointing.

Vella and I stared as the blue ball of light bounced across the field then over the horizon.

"Let's go," Vella said, following after it.

This time, I didn't argue.

Vella and I followed the light as it moved across the freshly-plowed fields. The light floated toward the back of the property. There was a stream between Madame Knightly's place and a neighbor's property.

The blue light danced toward the edge of the property. There, a thick tree branch had fallen over the wall. Frankie, excited to be on an adventure, climbed up the branch, stopping at the top to look back at us.

"We need to follow it. But Cricket, how are you?"

"I feel like I spent all night at a Cinco de Mayo party. But otherwise, I'm good. I can do it," I told her. "But Vella, how are we going to get back in? As soon as we cross the wall, we won't be able to find Witch Wood again without help."

Vella motioned to the light. "I'm not worried."

She was right. "Okay, let's go."

It took a good bit of balance, but I made my way across the fallen branch. Vella went ahead of me, climbing down with Frankie in her arms. When she got to the other side, she set the little dog down then helped me off, careful about my bad arm.

"You need to go easy. They had to give you stitches. Stop putting yourself in dangerous spots, please.

"I just couldn't let Zoey get bit. Dangerous spots? I am in the middle of the woods with you...*again*, following a weird blue light...*again*. Talk about dangerous spots."

"Last time, the blue light led us to Chase, Darius, and Ariel."

"And where are we headed now?" I asked.

Vella pointed. "Looks like we're crossing a stream."

I frowned as the blue light bounced over the stream then into the field adjacent to Witch Wood.

"Look," I said, turning back. Behind us was nothing more than a wall of mist. Witch Wood, which had been as plain as day the moment before, had vanished.

"The enchantment." Vella turned her attention back toward the orb of light. "There," Vella said, pointing to some stepping stones. "We can cross there."

Frankie stopped at the side of the stream to drink then went splashing on ahead of us.

Vella went first, holding onto my good hand to steady me. I was able to stay mostly out of the water, my foot slipping in only twice.

"Are you okay?" Vella asked when we reached the other side. "You look pale."

"My head and stomach are tumbling a bit."

Vella frowned then gazed after the light which danced between rows of dead cornstalks.

"Let's go," I told her.

"Are you sure?"

I nodded. "If there is something we need to see, let's go see it."

Vella nodded, and we went ahead. I didn't want to tell her that I felt like I might puke at any minute. But it didn't matter. We needed to go wherever the light was taking us. I didn't like that the world I lived in was full of weird spirits and such, but it was what it was. I'd about gotten used to it.

As we made our way through the corn field, some sort of weird sound came from the direction of Witch Wood. It almost sounded like an explosion.

Vella and I stopped. The mist around Witch Wood swirled strangely and then, all at once, dissipated. The mansion was clearly visible.

"Vella?" I said, worry clouding my voice.

"I see," she said. "Let's go."

"Something must be wrong. Tristan…we need to go back."

"No," Vella said. "Let's go," she said, and we turned and moved more quickly behind the blue light. The corn field provided us with good cover. Not a soul could see us in that field, if they had been looking.

My heart was pounding in my chest. What was happening at Witch Wood?

The walk felt like it took forever. My head swam, my chest thumped, my arm arched, and I damned near felt like puking the entire time. By the time we got out of the field, I felt like I might just drop.

"There," Vella said, watching as the blue light bounced across the driveway and through a thin crack in the barn door.

The dog ran ahead of us, slipping into the barn. Vella and I moved more carefully. Vella pushed the door open so we could go inside. The barn windows were old, dirty, and covered in cobwebs. Thin light shone in. I looked all around. There was nothing unusual here, just tractors and other farming equipment, a hayloft, grain bins, and animal pens. There was a small equipment room on one side. The blue light twinkled one last time then disappeared into the room.

Vella followed it, opening the door.

I sat down on a tractor tire and wiped the sweat off my brow. I took a couple of deep breaths and tried to calm my stomach.

"Well?" I called.

"Interesting," Vella answered.

"What's in there?"

"Guns. Lots and lots of guns."

A noise from outside startled us. It was followed by someone pushing the barn door open even more. Vella reappeared at once, holding what looked like an automatic weapon in her hands. I stood, realizing I had nothing on me, not even my pipe wrench. On top of that, my knees were just about ready to give out.

Vella lifted the gun, ready to shoot.

A moment later, Amelia, Zoey, and Layla walked in.

CHAPTER THIRTY-SEVEN

LAYLA

"LAYLA?" CRICKET SAID.

"Cricket? Vella? What are you doing here?" I asked, looking from one to the other. Amelia had led us down a woodland path to a property adjoining Witch Wood in the hopes we could get a look at what was happening.

"We could ask you the same," Vella replied.

"Witch Wood is compromised," I replied.

"The loft," Amelia said. "Maybe we can get a look from there."

"Binoculars inside," Vella said, motioning to the equipment room behind her.

"Cricket, you okay?" I asked. She looked deathly pale.

"Might throw up, but I'm not a zombie," she replied, bending over to take a deep breath.

"What happened?" I asked Vella.

She shook her head. "I don't know. We were outside. We were…led here. Next thing we knew, we heard an explosion at Witch Wood, and then the mist lifted."

"The town is crawling with the undead," I said. "That's where we were. There are so many."

"Just like at Claddagh-Basel," Cricket said.

"And in Hamletville before that."

"Then the kitsune have found us," Vella said.

"But what about Tristan, Logan, and Madame Knightly? I mean, they won't start anything with them," Cricket said.

"Who knows what the kitsune are capable of," I replied. "Tristan's people have honor. They don't. And now that their king is gone—"

"They will be out for blood," Vella finished for me.

"Where did you get that?" I asked her, looking at the gun she was holding.

She motioned over her shoulder. "Inside."

"I see movement," Zoey called from the loft above. "It's Logan and two strangers. The others are being led outside too."

"Others? All of them?" I asked, my heart beating hard. Kira and Susan were going to be terrified.

"Yes."

"We need to go. Now," I said. In the equipment room, I started pulling guns off the wall, digging through the boxes of ammo, loading them.

Amelia and Zoey climbed back down to join us.

"We need to get to our people before the undead get here," I said as I loaded the guns, handing them to the girls. Amelia looked at the weapon like she had no idea what to do with it.

"Okay," Vella said. "But how?"

"If we can take out the kitsune, I can pull up the enchantment around Witch Wood before the zombies arrive," Amelia said.

"How many kitsune were there?" I asked.

Zoey shook her head. "A lot. Maybe twenty or more people I didn't recognize."

We all looked at one another.

"We could try to bargain," Cricket offered.

"With them?" Vella said.

"Madame Knightly will try diplomacy, but in the end, she,

Tristan, and Logan will be forced to choose a side," I said.

"You know Tristan will protect us," Cricket said.

"Layla, what should we do?" Zoey asked.

I looked down at my blade. "We were not meant to survive this. We were not meant to live. But we have. We are alive. And we can survive the undead. The vampires are nearly decimated. The kitsune…they will never be satisfied until we are all dead. I killed their king, and I'll kill the rest of them too, or as many of them as I have to. We need to fight. If we give in now, we're as good as done, and I promised those little girls I'd protect them. I've lost everything else, but I'll die on my feet before I let a horde of zombies or some damned faerie people with a vengeance wipe out the last of my friends. We attack. We get everyone we can, then we head into the maze."

"To where?" Cricket asked.

"Home. To Hamletville."

"But then what?" Vella asked.

I looked at Cricket, remembering our conversation about Vella's cards. I smiled at Vella then motioned to Amelia. "Then, *the High Priestess.*"

CHAPTER THIRTY-EIGHT

LAYLA

"YOU GOING TO BE ALL RIGHT?" I asked Cricket as she checked her gun.

"Gotta save the living," she said, slipping a magazine into her weapon.

Adjusting the two automatics I had slung over my shoulders, I checked my boot daggers. Everything was ready.

"Who knew Mister Sanders had so many guns," Amelia said with a shake of the head. "He used to shoot clay pigeons. I would see him outside with a shotgun from time to time, but I didn't know he was—"

"A gun nut?" Zoey finished. "This should come in handy," she said, holding the sharp sickle she'd found on the barn wall.

"Oh yeah," I replied.

Zoey gave the blade a twirl. "Time for the harvesting."

I nodded. "Let's go."

With Amelia leading the way, we headed through the corn field toward the stream.

I needed to make this right. It couldn't go on like this anymore. We run. We're hunted. We run. We're hunted. We were better off dead. I had to make this end now. I knew what to do. I knew how to make this work. And I believed in the others. I cast a glance back at Cricket. If she could survive, we all could survive. I had to make this work.

"Grandma?" I whispered into the ether.

"See, Layla. See everything."

When we got to the wall, Amelia and Zoey climbed over first while Vella and I helped Cricket. Then I picked up Cricket's furry little companion.

"Careful," I told the little dog. "Foxes around," I said then steadied him on the branch before crossing.

I climbed over, meeting the others. I pulled my shashka. "They may have people scouting the perimeter. We need to avoid gunfire as long as possible."

"No machete, no wrench," Cricket said.

"And an arm full of stitches," Vella reminded her.

I cast a glance at Amelia. "I'm going to need you," I told her.

She nodded. "I know."

"Around the back, right?" I asked her.

"Keep to the back wall. We'll head to the rose garden. The lattice arbors will give us cover and a good line of sight."

I stepped in front of the others and moved quickly. Just as we were about to round past the grape arbors, I paused. In the distance, I saw a man walking the fence. His hair was brilliant red.

I looked back at Amelia who nodded, placing her hands together. She closed her eyes, concentrating, and then set her palms forward. She opened her eyes and nodded to me. I had no idea what she'd done, but the air around us seemed to shiver and all the hairs on the back of my neck rose.

Signaling the others to stay behind, I swept in low and fast on the kitsune. By the time he turned, it was too late.

"You," he managed to spit out before the shashka swung, the blade singing as it vibrated through the enchanted air. His head rolled to Zoey's feet.

"Gross," she said, kicking it into the weeds.

With a nod, we headed forward. We stayed low as we passed the grape vines. The vines sheltered us from view from the house. That, and whatever Amelia was doing. I couldn't see her magic at work, but the air all around was tingly.

When we reached the back of Witch Wood, we heard voices. Our people had been moved to the front of the house. We couldn't see them, but we could hear them.

Someone was shouting. Was it Tristan?

The stricken look on Cricket's face confirmed my suspicion.

"There," Amelia whispered, pointing to a path leading into the garden.

"Hey! Stop," someone called from behind us.

I looked back to see a kitsune woman come out of the vines. Zoey swept in on her, but the woman knocked the blade from her hand. I rushed to her aid, but Zoey swung around quickly and decked the woman with a right jab so strong the kitsune woman fell to her knees. I joined the fray and lopped off the kitsune woman's head.

When I turned back, I saw Amelia standing near the edge of the garden, concentrating hard.

"See. See everything."

It was then that I realized what she was doing. She was shifting the space around us, a little at a time, out of view of this world. Everything took on a strange vibration, like it was there and then it wasn't. She was opening up space in the otherworld, a space she herself was creating, so we could pass unseen.

"Let's go," she whispered.

We followed her into the rose garden then down a path that led us toward the back side of the house. We were able to see the others collected in the driveway.

"Everyone is outside," Vella whispered.

"The kitsune…there are eighteen of them," Zoey said.

"Who is she?" Cricket asked, pointing. We couldn't make out her words, but Tristan and a red-haired woman were in a fierce debate, Madame Knightly and Logan standing nearby.

Tom was holding Kira. Susan was holding onto her mother's leg. Both girls were crying. Rage swelled up in my chest.

"I don't know, and I don't care. Let's do this," I said then turned and scanned the back of the house. There, I saw what I was looking for: the propane tank.

"You sure everyone is outside?" I asked Vella.

"Yes."

"It's about to get really loud," I said, pointing toward the tank. I hoisted the gun I'd loaded with incendiary rounds and took aim. "Everyone ready? Cricket?"

"Grab our folks and head into the maze. Got it," she said. "Get ready, Frankie," she told the little dog.

"Just keep your dream in mind. It will take you where we need to go."

"We need to be fast. The noise will draw the zombies," Vella said.

"Amelia?"

"I'm ready."

"3…2…1."

Inhale.

Aim.

Fire.

The ground shook as the propane tank sitting along the back of the property behind Witch Wood exploded into a massive fireball. Glass shattered in both the greenhouse and the windows of Witch Wood. Part of the back wall behind the house exploded.

"What the hell," one of the kitsune screamed.

The kitsune rushed toward the explosion.

"Now," I yelled, and we headed across the back of the property toward them.

The first group, running to investigate the explosion, never even saw us emerge from the cover of the garden. Firing, Vella, Zoey, and I finished them where they stood. Their bodies crumpled onto the ground.

"It's her! Kill her," the red-haired woman screamed, pointing at me.

They turned toward us, weapons drawn.

We were vastly outnumbered.

But they weren't expecting Amelia.

"No," Amelia screamed, and with that strange magical force, she squinted her eyes hard and sent a wave of light toward them, knocking them off their feet. Dead or unconscious, I wasn't sure which, they fell to the ground.

I pulled my blade and rushed toward my people just as Chase threw his head back, slamming his skull into the nose of the kitsune man holding him. The man let him go at once. Chase turned and started kicking the kitsune man.

"Do something, you cows," the woman screamed at the kitsune soldiers around her. But her eyes were glued on Amelia.

I heard an arrow speed past my ear as I turned to see the remaining kitsune head my way. Chase ran toward Vella who cut loose the binds on his hands. She handed him a gun, and they rushed to free Darius and Kellimore.

Cricket moved in toward Frenchie and the girls while I made my way toward the woman who, I presumed, was the kitsune queen. As I raced across the grass, I saw that the first of the undead had made their way to Witch Wood.

"Layla?" Frenchie yelled as Cricket began to lead her and the others away.

"Frenchie, Cricket, go," I called then rushed the queen.

Cricket turned and she, Vella, Ariel, Elle, Frenchie, Will, who was holding Susan, and Tom, who had Kira, ran into the maze. The little dog followed quickly behind them.

Out of the corner of my eye, I saw Darius and Kellimore, along with the newcomers Brian and Brianna, fighting the remaining kitsune.

"Tristan," Cricket called, but he motioned for her to go as he hurried to join me.

Logan, leading Beatrice, ran after Cricket. Zoey grabbed Brian and Brianna, leading them away from the fight toward the maze.

"Stop them," the kitsune woman yelled, seeing they were about to make their escape.

Darius, Chase, and Kellimore moved quickly to intercept the kitsune who went after Cricket's group.

The kitsune woman, who'd been distracted, noticed that I was headed her way. Then she did something I hadn't expected. Moving quickly, she grabbed Madame Knightly roughly and put a blade to her throat.

"What are you doing?" Tristan yelled at her.

"Tell your bitch to put down her blade," the woman seethed.

"Layla," Tristan whispered aghast.

I looked behind me. Only Chase, Darius, Kellimore, and Amelia still remained. The kitsune lay dead or dying on the ground, and about a hundred zombies were closing in fast.

"Give her to me, and I'll give you this old bag of bones," the kitsune woman said through gritted teeth, glaring hard at me.

"Maeve, my dear, you're making a very big mistake," Madame Knightly said very calmly.

"Shut your mouth. I'm sick of your interference. We have won this battle. Mankind is dead. Why are you protecting these waifs?"

"Look around you," Tristan told her. "Your army was defeated before you even knew what was upon you. This is over."

"Never," the woman seethed. "Never. They must perish… all of them. I will bring *all* my people down on their heads if I must."

"No, I don't think so," Madame Knightly said. "In fact, from what I understand, not all your people agree with what you have done. And from what I hear, your sister did not condone your apocalypse."

"Who cares what she thinks, you old hag. I'm in charge."

"Isn't she heir to the throne of the unseelie after you?"

"Is that a threat? I'm not going anywhere, but I think *your* time is done," she said, pressing the blade to Madame Knightly's throat. A small trickle of blood dripped down her neck.

"Stop," Amelia cried out.

"Drop your sword," the kitsune woman told me, "or I kill her."

"No," Amelia replied for me. "Bastet," she called toward Madame Knightly.

Catching her meaning, Madame Knightly winked at Amelia and with a flash of light, shifted form. The small black cat slipped away from the kitsune woman. Amelia then flung her arms forward with so much force that I could see the blast of white light slam through the air toward the kitsune queen.

The woman screamed as the blast hit her, and she fell to

the ground.

Sweeping in quickly, I held my blade aloft, ready to strike off Maeve's head. But then I realized it wasn't necessary. Blood leaked from the kitsune woman's eyes and ears. She lay motionless.

"Look out," Kellimore yelled then began shooting at the undead who were now upon us.

Amelia picked up Bastet.

"To the maze! Quickly," I called.

Darius and Amelia, who was still holding the shape-shifted Madame Knightly, rushed toward the hedge. Chase, Tristan, and Kellimore rushed after them.

"Layla? Where are we going?" Tristan called to me.

"Everyone just think about Cricket. Follow Cricket and the others."

I shot into the massive horde of the undead as I wove back into the maze. A thick mist began to settle all around. As I backed deeper into the hedge, deep fog swirled all around me. I shot the undead tumbling toward me. There were so many of them.

"Here," I heard Tristan call to the others. "Turn this way. Now!" There was a flash of blue light from somewhere behind me and then there was silence.

They'd gone through the portal.

I was alone.

Aside from the gurgling sounds of the undead advancing through the maze, there was no other noise. Everyone was gone. Everyone would be back in Hamletville, with Cricket and Amelia, safe.

For a moment, I stopped.

The undead were just feet away, but I could feel their confusion. They were lost in the mist. And somewhere inside that crowd, I heard voices. Their strange words rattled in my head. The living undead walked among the rotted corpses. Were they talking to one another?

"Layla?" someone said then, grabbing my arm.

I turned to find Kellimore standing there, a confused and worried expression on his face.

"I waited for you. Come on. Let's go," he said. Taking my hand, he led me to the end of the maze where a strange blue light glimmered around a small circle of stones on the ground.

We stepped into the light and were immediately engulfed.

CHAPTER THIRTY-NINE

LAYLA

BY NOW, I'D GROWN USED TO THE STRANGE FORCE hurtling me through the in-between spaces. When I landed with a thud, I didn't think anything of it. My shashka bounced from my hands across the leaf-strewn ground.

"Are you all right?" Tristan asked, offering me a hand up.

"Layla," Susan called, running to me, her sister following behind her. The girls wrapped their arms around my waist.

"Is everyone all right?" I asked. "Cricket?" I said, turning to her. I saw she was leaning on Vella and pale as ever.

"I'm okay but wouldn't mind getting off my feet."

Kellimore retrieved my blade and handed it to me.

I smiled at him, fully aware of the fact that he'd waited for me. The implications weren't lost on me.

Madame Knightly, who had shifted back into human form, turned to me. "I must thank you," she said then. "Now, I presume you know where you are?"

"Yes. Home," I replied then turned to Tom, Will, and Frenchie.

"Home? Hamletville home?" Tom asked, looking around with assessing eyes.

"We're in Fox Hollow, back behind my property."

"Nice name," Chase said.

I smirked. All things considered, he was right.

"Very well," Madame Knightly said then signaled to Logan and Tristan. "You'll need to excuse us. As you can imagine, these changes present some challenges for us. We must consult with our people."

I nodded. "Follow the stream into the woods. It's thinnest there. That's where I've seen Peryn."

Madame Knightly nodded then turned and walked away.

Logan squeezed Amelia's hand then followed behind the ancient matriarch. Tristan and Cricket exchanged low words, but eventually I heard Cricket say, "Don't worry. I'll be all right."

Tristan frowned, then turned to follow the others. He paused when he got to me. "Nightfall. You must be cautious. You're still not alone."

"I know," I told him. "I have a plan."

"I expected no less," he said then followed Madame Knightly and Logan into the woods.

I turned back to the others. "Follow me. My house is just this way," I said, leading them through the woods.

"Oh Mommy, are we really back home?" Kira asked.

"Yes, I think so," Frenchie told her.

"But what about those bad vampires? They won't come back for us, will they?" Susan asked.

"No," Frenchie said, but the tremor in her voice told me she wasn't entirely sure.

Frenchie didn't know it, but it was a lie. If my grandmother's words were true, there were already vampires in Hamletville. And they were waiting for us. But I had a plan. With a little luck, I could finish this mess once and for all.

"So, a plan, huh?" Will asked, falling into step with me. "Seems like you might need someone familiar with Hamletville to help."

"Make that two someones," Tom offered.

I smiled at them. "I thought you'd never ask."

* * *

Tom, Will, Chase, Zoey, Kellimore, and I stood outside the gate of my grandmother's property. Well, at least we thought we were standing outside the gate. Amelia had cast a powerful spell rendering the property invisible, just as it had been at Witch Wood. A heavy fog covered the space where the fence should have been.

"How will she know when to let us back in?" Will asked.

I shook my head. "She won't. When the sun comes up, we go home."

"Well, this should be fun," Chase said.

"I didn't tell you to come," I said with a smirk.

"No, but Cricket did," he said with a laugh.

"Now what?" Tom asked.

"We have about five hours before sundown. We need to pick off any stray undead roaming around. I don't know about you, but I don't want to fight vampires and the undead at the same time."

"Have the syringes?" Zoey asked.

I nodded. Beatrice had managed to escape Witch Wood with a tote full of supplies, including the vaccine, Doctor Gustav's notes, and the undead blood.

"All right, let's head over to Tom's," I said then got into my Range Rover. To my relief, it started with no problem. It seemed like ages since we'd left Hamletville, but in reality, only a couple of weeks had passed. When the world unfolds, it does it fast.

"So, all of you have seen these vampires before? For real?"

Zoey asked.

"Unfortunately," Will answered.

"There was a hive of them living on an island in the Great Lakes. They were hunting people. They found us," I explained.

"And we were stupid enough to go with them. Look at us now," Tom said. "Layla, we should have listened to you."

I shook my head. "There was no escaping them. Even if we hadn't gone to the Harpwind, they'd found us."

"Do you think any of Rumor's vampires survived?" Will asked.

"They had very little time to get to land before the sun came up, and Sarah, the one who showed up at Claddagh-Basel, said their numbers were decimated."

"Until we decimated her," Will said.

Kellimore laughed. "I've seen a lot of shit, but *that* was gross."

"What about other stuff that's supposed to work against vampires? You know, garlic, stake through the heart, holy water?" Zoey asked.

"Holy water?" I pulled out a small plastic gun from my pocket. "Yeah, it works."

Zoey shook her head in disbelief, her blue eyes wide.

I turned the SUV onto Main Street. So far there were only two undead wandering the streets aimlessly. I slowed, and Chase and Kellimore got out, killing the mindless creatures. I turned down Ash Street toward Tom's house which sat along the lake. I parked the SUV, and we all got out. Tom and I went to his garage.

"It feels surreal," he said, bending to lift the mat in front of his garage door. Underneath was the key. "I can't wrap my head around it. It feel strange to be home."

He was right. The moment I stepped onto the property

on Fox Hollow Road, I'd felt the same way. We were back, but so many of us were missing. We'd lost nearly everyone. "We made it back, but—"

"But without the others."

I nodded.

"Well, at least Cricket's group and Amelia's group are safe. We did something right, I guess."

I smiled at Tom. It moved me to think that I wasn't the only one who shared a sense of responsibility. Perhaps that was how we'd made it this far. Maybe all of us felt accountable for the rest.

I followed Tom inside. The garage housed two trucks, two ATVs, a dirt bike, and a lot of tools. Tom took two sets of keys off the wall, handing one to me.

"Try the Ford," he said, heading toward the other pickup.

I slipped behind the wheel of Tom's lovingly restored 1950s truck. I'd seen him drive it around town a few times, showcasing his hobby. As usual, the light blue truck was waxed to a glimmering polish.

I turned the ignition. The truck's engine rods knocked then rumbled to a start.

Tom got out and opened the garage doors then waved to me to pull out. He pulled the second truck out behind me. I got out of the vehicle and joined the others.

"Okay, let's split up," I said. "Will, you go with Chase. Tom, you take Kellimore. I'll go with Zoey. The town looks pretty good, just some strays, but we need to be sure. We'll meet at the elementary school at five o'clock," I said, handing watches to the others.

"Where'd you get these?" Will asked.

"They were Grandma's."

With a smile, Will nodded. "She thought of everything."

"Layla, the vampires..." Tom began but was uncertain what to say.

"I'm told there are three of them haunting Hamletville."

"How do you know that?" Chase asked.

"The spirits told me," I said with a half-smile.

"Now you do sound like Grandma Petrovich," Tom said.

I grinned. "If you get into trouble, head back to the school." I handed the keys to Tom. "Will, you take east of Morrigon Hill Road. Tom, you take west. Zoey and I will have a look around at the pier and downtown."

Tom passed off a set of keys to Will then motioned for Kellimore to get into his vintage truck with him.

Kellimore stopped as he passed me. "Hey, you be safe, okay? Keep an eye out for Swamp Thing."

"He's got nothing on me," I said with a smile.

"Of course not."

"You be safe too," I said with a soft smile.

I saw the effect of the glance on Kellimore, and I liked it. I waved to him then climbed into the SUV with Zoey. When I turned to look at her, she smirked and raised an eyebrow at me.

"What?" I asked.

"Nothing," she said with a smile then looked out the window. "So, zombies, kitsune, and vampires. Awesome. Anything else trying to kill us?"

"Infection, starvation, nuclear fallout—"

"I'm sorry I asked. It's like we don't belong here anymore. You get that feeling too?"

"Yeah," I said with a nod. "I do."

"So what now?"

"Well," I said, looking at the watch, "for the next two hours, we hunt zombies. After that, we hunt vampires. And if we survive the night, we'll see what the faerie people have decided to do with us."

"Fabulous," Zoey said as she flipped through my CDs. "You know, you should have upgraded to MP3s."

"Should have," I said. "But aren't you glad I didn't?"

She lifted my old Tool *Lateralus* CD and slipped it into the player. "That I am," she said with a smirk then hit play.

CHAPTER FORTY

AMELIA

I STOOD IN THE DRIVEWAY studying the fence. The sun was dipping lower and lower in the sky. Night was coming. If I had done what Madame Knightly had taught me to do, then we were safe here, at least for tonight. I had not seen the vampires, and I didn't want to. As it was, my world was completely flipped upside down. Adding another violent force into my field of awareness was more than I could handle. The world already looked so strange. Something was changing. It was like the hue on everything was getting darker. And I was getting more powerful. The magic inside me scared me. I was humbled and grateful that I'd been strong enough to save Cricket, to protect Madame Knightly, but I had failed to save my own mother. In the end, I'd lost her twice. My heart grieved.

"Amelia? Are you all right?" I turned to find Vella coming toward me.

I nodded then looked at the valley behind the property. Wherever Logan, Madame Knightly, and Tristan had gone, they hadn't come back. Maybe they never would. I didn't know.

"Yeah, just worried about...everyone."

Vella linked her arm in mine. "Don't worry," she said matter-of-factly.

"No?" I asked, turning to study her and the glimmering

purple aura that always surrounded her.

"What's the use?" she asked with a half-smile. "Come tomorrow morning, we will know one way or another."

I nodded. "Layla, Zoey, all of them. They're strong. They'll be all right."

"How is your fence?"

"Good, I think."

"Your fence has me wondering."

"About?"

"Tristan's people. Once, they lived in the same world as mankind. And then they separated from us."

"The veil between the worlds."

"What's the difference between that veil and what you've done here?" Vella asked, motioning to the fence.

"I guess just scale."

Vella nodded, patted my arm, and turned to head back inside. But she stopped for just a moment first. "We cannot survive in the dead world. Our world is gone. We don't belong here anymore."

"Then what should we do?" I asked.

She raised an eyebrow at me. "If only we knew how to drop a veil between our world—all of our world—and the dead world. If only there was someone with a gift like that."

"Vella?" I whispered aghast. Surely she didn't think I was capable of something of that magnitude. "It's too much, too large. I don't know how."

"You are the High Priestess. You stand between the worlds. If you don't know how, then no one does," she said then went back inside.

CHAPTER FORTY-ONE

LAYLA

I PULLED MY SUV INTO THE PARKING LOT AT THE PIER. There were two undead roaming around, looking completely lost and very rotted. Zoey took out the first while I killed the second.

I glanced down the pier. My dirt bike was still sitting under the shelter. No new boats were docked.

"I'm going to go take a look," I said, motioning toward the pier.

Zoey nodded.

I headed down the wooden planks to the end of the pier then checked all around. There were no boats in the water, at least none that were visible, and no boats docked along the shoreline either. Not that anyone was planning to hide in plain sight, but if Rumor's people had found another way to escape, if they'd had another boat we hadn't seen, then maybe. But there was nothing.

I glanced around one last time, my eyes falling on the Fisherman's Wharf, the restaurant where I'd found Jamie's gift, the flower of life medallion. I lowered the binoculars and stared out at the lake. The dark waves lapped against the rocky shoreline. It wasn't supposed to end this way. I was supposed to get my happily ever after with the man I loved. Now, he was gone. Not just dead, but undead, and gone.

I headed back to Zoey who waited in the parking lot cleaning the goo off her sickle.

"Anything?" she asked.

I shook my head. "Let's check town."

Driving back toward Main Street, Zoey and I made a slow canvas of the town.

"It's quiet," Zoey said. "Not like Brighton. You guys got the windows all boarded up?"

"We were surviving here. Let me show you," I said then turned down River Run Drive to the spot where the bridge used to be. The crumbled remains of the bridge hung out over the water.

"Whoa," Zoey said. "What happened there?"

"We blew up the bridge. It was the main route into town from the outside world. Between the river and the lake, we were protected. We barricaded the other street coming into town. Everywhere else was just rural. We were safe, for a while."

"Until the vampires."

"It was the kitsune. They led the vampires to us. And just like in Brighton, and at Claddagh-Basel before that, they led the undead as well."

"Why do the kitsune hate us so much?"

"We trashed our world. It was their job to protect it. So they trashed us."

Zoey shook her head.

I put the SUV into reverse then drove back into town, turning onto a back street. Everything looked the same. There was, as far as I could tell, almost nothing out of place. But the undead were still roaming the streets. There weren't many, but there were enough to notice. Again and again, Zoey and I stopped and finished the meandering undead. None of the walking corpses who had found their way to Hamletville were like Elizabeth or Caroline, the thinking undead. These were just corpses.

Driving back across town, I suddenly realized with a heart-paining twang that we were near Jamie's house. I slowed as we passed. Then I saw something off. I stopped the SUV.

"What is it?" Zoey asked.

"The door is open. It wasn't before."

"Wind, maybe?"

I shook my head then got out.

I pulled my shashka, and we crossed the lawn slowly, eyeing everything around us. There were no undead anywhere. And there were no kitsune, at least not that we'd seen yet.

"Hello? Who's in there?" I whispered in my mind.

Nothing. No answer.

"Layla?" Zoey asked.

"I don't see—or hear—anything. But still, something's off here."

Zoey nodded.

I swallowed hard, realizing a terrible possibility.

What if it was Jamie?

Holding my sword in front of me, I stepped slowly inside. Bending, I felt the carpet at the entrance. It was dry, and there were no leaves inside. However the door had gotten open, it had been opened recently. The smell inside the house took me back. It was like I was with Jamie. I was completely overcome by his scent. It made my heart ache.

"Hello?" I called, using my mind.

There was no answer.

"Who's in here?" I called.

There was an odd sound coming from the back of the house, like someone had knocked something over.

Zoey followed me inside. I motioned for her to check the

kitchen while I headed toward the back. I slid my sword into its scabbard and reached for my gun. Zoey pulled hers as well.

The kitchen and living room clear, Zoey and I headed toward the back of the house. Again, I heard a thumping sound. It was coming from the spare bedroom. My heart slammed in my chest. A million thoughts spun through my mind, the worst imagining it was Jamie.

"Jamie?" I called lightly.

From behind the door, something crashed.

"Dammit," I said then pushed the door open.

With a hiss and a low growl, a raccoon jumped out of a cardboard box and scrambled up Jamie's gun cabinet, knocking down some of his old high school trophies in the process. It was greedily holding a pack of dried noodles in its mouth, growling at us at the same time.

"Christ, scared the piss out of me," Zoey said.

I holstered my gun as the raccoon climbed up through a broken ceiling tile into the attic.

"Okay. Just a raccoon. But he didn't open the door, right? I mean, they're smart but not that smart," Zoey said.

"Yeah," I agreed. "Maybe one of the guys was by."

"Sure, maybe," Zoey said, but I could see she was unnerved too.

I looked at my watch. It was four-thirty. "We need to finish up," I said.

Zoey nodded, and we went back outside.

As we were leaving, however, something caught my eye. Lying on the coffee table was the very charm I'd given to Jamie. I froze. Hadn't he attached it to his knife? I tried to remember. Did he have that knife at the Harpwind? At Claddagh-Basel? Maybe he'd left the charm behind. After all, we'd fought just before we went to the Harpwind. Maybe he'd taken it off.

Scooping it up, I slipped the flower of life medallion into my pocket. My eyes welled with tears.

"You okay?" Zoey asked.

"Yeah. This…this was my fiancé's house."

"Sorry," Zoey said, setting her hand on my shoulder.

"Thanks." I pulled the door shut behind me, realizing then that the door wasn't fitting tightly in the frame anymore. I locked the door from the inside and pulled it shut. If I managed to see the next sunrise, I'd come back to fix the door, keeping Jamie's memory locked up and safe.

CHAPTER FORTY-TWO

LAYLA

AS I PULLED THE RANGE ROVER INTO THE elementary school parking lot, Will and Chase pulled in behind me. Kellimore and Tom were standing outside.

"Layla," Tom said, opening my door. "Problem."

"What's wrong?" I asked, looking from Tom to Kellimore.

"We know where they are," Kellimore said.

"What?" Chase asked.

"We drove through the cemetery at the Catholic Church. Someone tampered with the Zurn mausoleum," Tom said, referring to the largest and oldest crypt.

"Tampered how?" I asked.

"Door had been opened. We could see the scrape marks on the pavement. We didn't investigate closely. But…" Tom said then paused.

"There were bodies outside. They were like husks, just lying around everywhere," Kellimore said.

"If they aren't there anymore, and we bet our money on that place, we're screwed if they find us," Will said.

"They're in there," Tom said. "You could feel it, that terrible feeling you get in the pit of your stomach when something's wrong."

I looked up at the sky. The sun was starting to slant toward dusk.

"Salt," I said. "We need salt and gas. We'll ring the place with salt, trapping them inside, then set it on fire."

"There is more salt than you could ever need in the cafeteria," Tom said.

"Chase and I can go round up the gasoline. We'll meet you over there," Will said.

"Any chance Jeff left us a couple of bottles down at Figgy's?" I asked.

Tom smiled sadly. Jeff had been an ass, and had nearly gotten us killed, but he'd been one of us. "Maybe some gin. He wasn't a gin drinker. I'm guessing I should grab bar towels too?"

I nodded. "And vodka, if you see any."

"Vodka?"

"Because if I need to fight vampires, in a graveyard, at night, I could use a drink."

Despite the underlying tension, everyone laughed.

"Lady wants a drink, son. Best get on it," Chase said, clapping Kellimore on the shoulder. He turned and waved to Will. The two of them took off.

"We'll grab the salt," I told Zoey.

"The undead don't scare me. They're mindless. The idea of a vampire, and not the sorry-assed sparkly kind, terrifies me. It's the deception. That's what makes them so freaking scary," Zoey said.

"Yes," I replied, thinking of what happened to Ian once he'd turned. The vampire blood had unleased his shadow aspect, and it was terrifying.

I opened the door to the gymnasium. The scent of cleaning fluids and dust, the familiar smell of the place, sent my mind spinning. Here I was again. Sitting just inside the door was a table with supplies, including flashlights. I grabbed two, clicked them on, and then we headed inside.

"The cafeteria pantry still had some supplies, mostly spices and other things left that we didn't have a lot of use for or didn't know what to do with, including salt. Ethel, another one of our people, always found a way to make something though."

Zoey shook her head. "Sometimes I can't believe this is happening. It's too impossible."

I understood her feeling of disbelief. "I try not to think about it, not to feel any of it. It's the only way I can keep going."

"It's going to catch up with you eventually, you know."

"Yeah. But not today," I said as we headed into the cafeteria. When we got there, however, it quickly became apparent that we had a problem. The place was flooded. "Shit," I said with a sigh, pulling open the door to the pantry. Running along the top of the wall was a set of pipes that led into the kitchen. One of the pipes had burst and was shooting water everywhere. Every box, every item, was soaking wet and turning green.

"What happened?" Zoey asked. "You guys had water?"

"It's part of the old well system. This end of the school was built in the eighteen-hundreds. In the spring the old well overflows. We weren't here to fix it. I remember the janitors fighting with the lines every spring when I was a kid. Here," I said, handing her my flashlight. "Pan it up there," I said, pointing to a faucet.

Carefully climbing up the slippery shelves, I reached out and turned the faucet, squeezing it shut. A moment later, the water stopped spurting.

I climbed back down. "Great," I said, scanning the room. "Totally soaked. Probably even dissolved," I said, pointing to the cardboard containers of salt sitting in—and half floating—

on the bottom shelf. "And our plan doesn't work without salt. It's the only thing that will keep them locked in."

"You guys have a municipal building? In Brighton, they always salted the roads in the winter. I remember my dad bitching about them not using enough salt."

"We should. I mean, it was nearly winter, and I don't think anyone ever bothered with it. We used snowmobiles and even a sleigh."

"No shit. Crafty. I was stuck all winter watching Amelia and Logan fall in love while I half died of boredom and loneliness, wondering if I was ever going to see another guy again."

"Well, I brought you some options. You're welcome."

Zoey laughed. "Thanks."

We left and drove across town. I realized then that the time was starting to get the better of us. The sun dipped lower on the horizon. As soon as dusk set in, the vampires would begin to wake. Zoey and I were going to have to work quickly if we wanted to get back to the cemetery in time.

I pulled the Range Rover into the parking lot of the municipal building. The administrative offices sat on the first floor. In a basement below were the equipment rooms and garage which let out onto the alleyway behind the building. If I remembered correctly, the salt was stored in the garage below. When everything had fallen apart, someone had boarded up the windows on the municipal building. They'd found some undead inside during our initial sweep of the town. After that, we'd just locked up the building with a chain.

"We'll need to go downstairs," I told Zoey as we approached the door. "We'll get the garage open, see if there are any trucks down there that will start. Otherwise, we'll just pull the SUV around."

Zoey nodded, but her brow was furrowed.

"What is it?" I asked.

She shook her head. "Just a weird feeling."

When we got to the door, Zoey's weird feeling made sense. The chain around the door handle was gone. I tried the door. It opened easily.

"Okay," I said slowly. "That's not right. The door used to have a chain."

"Maybe we should get the guys," Zoey said, eyeing the building.

I looked up at the sky. The sun was already beginning to drop toward the lake. I shook my head. "We're running out of time."

"Shit. Yeah. I know. Okay, well, let's go see," she said then pulled her gun.

Reaching inside my vest, I pulled out the little water gun filled with holy water and handed it to her. "Just in case."

"Great."

I pulled my shashka and we crept inside. With the windows boarded shut, the place was completely dark. There was a spray of blood on the wall near the reception area. I motioned to Zoey to follow me as we turned left and moved down the hallway toward the back stairwell. The place had a sharp smell. The musty and decaying scent assailed my nose. Zoey snapped on her flashlight. With the office doors all closed, the only light from outside was that coming in from the front door. The back of the building was dark and silent.

"Let's check the rooms," I whispered.

My shashka ready, Zoey's gun drawn, one by one we opened the office doors. Signs of struggle were apparent, desks overturned, papers lying everywhere, but there was no sign of anyone. But Zoey was right. Something felt strange here.

"Let's go downstairs," I whispered.

The rooms clear, we exited the first floor and descended the back stairwell. The stairwell was dimly-lit by a battery-powered exit sign.

As we rounded the stairs, my heart started beating harder. Something wasn't right here. Something was off.

"Hey," Zoey said, shining her flashlight on the wall. "There's a fallout shelter here?"

I followed the beam of light. On the wall was a sign for an emergency shelter. There were two in town, one here and one at the library, but they were old and empty. The one in the library had been used for storage. Ian's group had checked out the one here. I hadn't even remembered it.

"I…I think we need to hurry," I said, my stomach twisting into a knot.

Zoey nodded then pushed open the door. We went inside the garage.

"Let's get the garage doors open. Quickly," I said, but then I paused. Inside my head, I heard muttering voices. I heard conversation, but could not make out the words. I'd heard such chatter before.

Seeing the impression on my face, Zoey stopped. "Layla?

From somewhere in the back of the garage, I heard chains rattle and the sound of a door slowly opening.

"Oh shit," Zoey said, then turned and ran toward the garage door.

Moving backward toward Zoey, my blade poised and ready, my eyes searched the darkness. There was a strange smell in the room and a weird chill like someone had left a refrigerator door open. Had they been in the fallout center? Had they been hiding here? But if they were here, what was in the cemetery?

"Is that you, Miss Katana?" I heard a woman ask. She had

a heavy accent. It wasn't Rumor. The voice lacked the seductive purr, but I'd heard this voice before. "We've been waiting for the bogatyrka to come home. How nice of you to come to us."

"Layla, the door is too heavy. I can't lift it," Zoey said, panic filling her voice.

Moving quickly, I turned and pushed, but something was wrong. I scanned my flashlight above to discover the mechanism above the door was broken.

"Can we make it back to the stairs?" Zoey whispered.

"No, you cannot," a male voice called from the back of the room.

That made two of them. How many more?

Taking Zoey by the arm, I pulled her to the next garage door. We heaved hard, but the door didn't budge.

Motioning, I pointed toward the exit sign above the main door.

"Where are you going, bogatyrka? Don't you want to see what the sunlight did to my pretty face?" the woman called.

I flashed my light toward the back of the garage in time to see a familiar face with blonde hair. It was Katya, Rumor's main henchman at the Harpwind. The skin on one side of her face was completely scorched, and her eye drooped. She grinned wildly then disappeared, fluttering away from my beam of light.

"I don't think she missed you," another female voice called from the darkness.

That made three.

"But I've been waiting for her all this time. I wanted to show her what her handiwork did. Those of us who survived the Harpwind barely made it to that abandoned tanker in time. And even then, not all of us survived. The sun scorched many of my comrades, and gave me this beauty mark. But I am glad you're here now. How did you know where to find us? We thought for certain you'd find the little surprise we left for you in the cemetery."

My heart beat hard. "What surprise?"

She laughed but didn't answer.

I moved quietly and carefully toward the door. Clearly, we were in trouble. But so were the others.

I took a deep breath and reached for Zoey's hand. Moving slowly, I snapped off her flashlight then turned off mine as well. I dropped the light then reached into my pocket and pulled out a syringe. Holding the shashka in one hand and a syringe in the other, I moved toward the door.

"You're not coming this way, are you?" a voice called from the direction of the door. I swished the shashka in front of me while pulling Zoey against me, lining us up back to back.

My senses told me they were close. Too close.

"See. See everything."

I took a deep breath and listened. I could hear them talking.

"Block her."

"I've got her. They're headed this way."

"Get her. Now!"

"Zoey, shoot the gun I gave you," I screamed, lunging forward into the darkness with a slashing movement. My blade connected with something hard, and I heard the male grunt.

Nearby, a woman screamed.

"What is this? What have you done?"

Zoey snapped on her flashlight to see a female vampire writhing on the floor near her. She sprayed the woman again. The vampire screamed out in agony. There was a sharp smell of sulfur in the air as the female vampire melted.

On the ground in front of me, the male vampire grabbed

his side then rose. His wound was healing. Moving fast, I spun my blade toward his head, but he morphed into shadow and retreated.

Grabbing Zoey by the arm, I ran toward the door and flung it open. Dim sunlight shimmered above the lake. Ruby red and burnt orange colors illuminated the skyline. We were too late to help the guys.

A moment later, the two vampires appeared at the door.

"Run," I told Zoey.

The male vampire gritted his teeth and burst out of the door. He hit Zoey with such force that the little water gun flew out of her hand and tumbled across the parking lot.

"Layla! Help," Zoey yelled.

In the dying sunlight, the vampire smoldered, wisps of black smoke rising off him, but he didn't die. I flicked the cap off the needle and raced toward the vampire as Zoey struggled to evade his bite. Heaving my hand up, I slammed the syringe into his back and pressed the plunger. Suddenly another body smacked into me, and I tumbled to the side.

Catching my footing as quickly as possible, I held my shashka tightly and spun on Katya. Like the male vampire, she too burned in the dimming sunlight. But she didn't seem to care. She gritted her fanged teeth and lunged at me. I swiped my sword. She was so fast. I twirled my blade over my head then slashed. Katya swept in and bashed me hard in the stomach. I stumbled back among a clutch of pine trees. She advanced on me, now sheltered from the sun by the shade.

"Katya, stop this. We never wanted any trouble from you. Just leave us. You don't have to die," I told her.

"I cannot leave you. Don't you understand? This isn't about revenge. It's about survival. Without your blood, we're dead. I hate you, but I need you to survive."

From behind us, the vampire man screamed loudly. Zoey pushed him off then jumped to the side. The man convulsed on the pavement as Zoey stood over him. A moment later, Zoey took out her gun and shot him in the head.

Distracted by the scene, I was startled when Katya screamed loudly and lunged at me. But this time, she was stopped in her tracks as one of the undead burst through the trees and grabbed her, knocking her to the ground. Katya howled as the undead man bit into her throat. Her scream died with a gurgle of blood. Zoey ran toward me. She lifted her gun and aimed it at the undead man who rose the moment Katya's feet went still.

Then, realization washed over me.

Moving quickly, I pushed Zoey's hand aside a fraction of a second before she pulled the trigger.

Bark flew off a tree nearby.

The undead man turned then, blood dripping off his chin, and looked at me.

"Jamie?" I whispered.

CHAPTER FORTY-THREE

LAYLA

"LAYLA," JAMIE WHISPERED IN MY MIND.

"How did you get here?"

"The mist. I got lost in the mist. I was…confused. And then I ended up here."

"Jamie?" I said softly, stepping toward him. It was him but not him. His skin was white, as were his eyes. The blood around his mouth was a gruesome sight. My heart hurt so badly, pain squeezing my chest.

"Layla, be careful," Zoey cautioned.

"She's right. I'm not…I'm not the same. I think the doctor—"

"She infected you. I know. We tried her cure on another… like you. It doesn't work on those who've already turned."

"Layla. It hurts. The hunger. I can't…I'm not safe. I'm not the same. Please shoot me."

"No. I can't," I whispered.

"The vampires were waiting for you. I watched them. I knew you would come home. I waited for you. I just wanted you to be safe. Please, please end it."

"Jamie, I love you. I can't."

"Her," he said, motioning to Zoey.

"Oh, please don't ask that."

"Layla," Zoey said, looking sadly at Jamie. It was clear that she'd read between the lines.

"Don't let me go on like this. I don't want to hurt anyone. I can barely control it. I can't go on like this."

"Zoey, go start the SUV. We need to get to the cemetery. The others are in danger," I said, tossing the keys to her.

"Are you…"

"I'm coming."

She took the keys then left, leaving me and Jamie alone.

"You're not gone. You're still here. You're still you."

"No. It's taking everything I have inside me not to attack you, not to eat you. The desire is nearly overwhelming," he said. I saw that he was trembling. *"Please end it."*

Tears streamed down my cheek. I pulled my gun from the back of my jeans and aimed it at him.

"It wasn't supposed to end like this," I said, my voice weak. My hands shook as tears rolled down my cheeks. "How can I let you go?"

"You must. Live, Layla. That's what you can do for me."

"I can't do it."

"Layla, I'm already dead. Don't let me suffer like this." Jamie closed his eyes. *"I love you, Layla."*

"I love you too," I whispered, and then I pulled the trigger.

CHAPTER FORTY-FOUR

LAYLA

WE DROVE QUICKLY ACROSS TOWN. The sun had already set by the time we got to the cemetery. We'd just passed the cemetery gates when we heard a massive boom and saw an explosion of orange light. Flames shot up from among the trees. As I drove the SUV toward the mausoleum, I watched in horror as at least two dozen undead, most of whom were now on fire, filtered out of the open door of the tomb.

"It was a trap," Zoey said, aghast. "There were undead inside. Nice distraction for the humans so the vampires could have easily picked us off."

I nodded absently then grabbed my gun and headed across the cemetery toward the others. Will, Kellimore, Chase, and Tom were shooting and falling back toward their trucks as the undead advanced on them. Zoey and I quickly joined the fray. The heat coming off the undead bodies and the terrible stench of roasted flesh gagged me. But I felt nothing. I moved automatically. My mind was numb. I couldn't, wouldn't think about what had just happened.

Jamie had come home.

Jamie had saved me.

And I'd killed him.

I couldn't let it in. There was no way I could survive the pain. It was too terrible. I choked the anguish that wanted to overwhelm me and took aim, shooting one undead creature after another. Soon, there was nothing left but heaps of bodies lying in the graveyard, smoldering down to charred husks.

By chance, the vampires' ruse had failed.

Or maybe it was something more.

Maybe it was fate.

Maybe.

But it hardly mattered.

The undead still walked. Vampires still lived. And the kitsune still hated us.

We might survive this night, but what next?

I headed back to my SUV. Opening the trunk, I sat down and looked out at the night's sky. Save the glow coming from the dying flames on the corpses, it was dark. I stared at the curves of the mountains, black silhouettes against the night's sky. A canvas of twinkling stars hung overhead.

Some time passed before I heard someone approach.

It was Kellimore.

He sat down beside me and handed me something.

I looked down to find half a bottle of vodka. I twisted the cap off and took a massive swig and then another.

I handed the bottle to Kellimore but then paused. "Are you even old enough to drink?"

"Close enough," he said then took the bottle, taking a draught.

He handed the bottle back to me.

I closed my eyes. Tears streamed down my cheeks. I took another drink, then another, then another. We sat there for the longest time. I didn't want to feel anything anymore. I didn't want to remember any of this.

"Come on," Kellimore said, taking my hand. "We're going to go back to Tom's house to wait out the night. Zoey told us what happened. Layla, I'm so sorry."

"Yeah. Thanks," I said absently then slid out of the SUV. I swooned, leaning hard on Kellimore.

"Maybe I should take this," Kellimore said, reaching out for my shashka.

"My scabbard," I mumbled, fumbling to unhook my belt. I shook my head and took another drink.

"I can get it, if that's okay," he said carefully.

I nodded.

Kellimore moved delicately as he unhooked the buckle on my belt. Feeling him so close to me, all I wanted to do was fall against him and weep. How good he'd felt that day at Witch Wood. How safe I'd felt in his arms. How freaking messed up it was that I felt like that, in the midst of all this misery. I was ashamed that my mind could toy with such ideas after what had just happened.

Kellimore slid my shashka into the scabbard then closed the trunk. Taking me carefully by the arm, he helped me into the Range Rover. He went and spoke to the others then returned once more.

We drove away from the cemetery. Wordlessly, I watched out the window as we drove through town. We passed the library, the old diner where I'd lived with my mother in the upstairs apartment, Ian's shop, all the sights and scenes of home illuminated only by the moonlight. I felt so hollow. Everything felt so hollow. I drank the vodka, holding the sharp liquid in my mouth, savoring the burning sensation as it trickled down my throat. I closed my eyes and let the drink dull my senses. I didn't want to feel.

When I opened my eyes again, Kellimore was helping me out of the Range Rover and guiding me toward Tom's house. The others smiled sympathetically at me.

"There is a spare room in the back," Tom said. "You got her?"

"Yeah," Kellimore replied.

"Will and I will be back in a bit," Tom said. "We can't leave Jamie there like that. We'll be back soon."

"Zoey and I will keep watch," Kellimore said.

Kellimore led me to a back bedroom then sat me down on the bed. My whole world was spinning. Everything seemed far away. There was this odd feeling inside me, like misery and joy were on a swing set connected to my heart, both of them pumping hard. Kellimore leaned my shashka against the footboard. Then, moving carefully, he took the vodka bottle from my hands.

"Hey, I was drinking that," I complained. My head was swimming, and the words coming out of my mouth didn't sound like my own.

"I know," Kellimore replied with a chuckle. "Put a dent in it. You're holding your liquor for the moment. Better stop now before you end up with alcohol poisoning."

"I'm Russian. That's not going to happen."

Kellimore smiled. "Then how about you stop before you do something stupid."

"Something stupid?" I asked with a laugh. "Like what?"

Kellimore looked at me. In the dim moonlight, he smiled. "Who knows? Start hunting werewolves?"

I laughed then reached out and touched the scar on his face. "Kellimore?" I whispered softly.

"Or that," he said, then pulled back. "Or that."

"But I thought…"

"When you're sober. And if you really mean it. Then that, all of that, but not right now. Rest, Layla. We'll wake you when the sun comes up," he said then helped me lie down. He gently covered me and then left. Tears streamed down my cheeks. I closed my eyes.

"Tu-tu-tu, Layla," I heard a voice say then.

I opened my eyes just a crack to see the ethereal form of my grandmother sitting on the edge of the bed.

"Cheap vodka loosens the lips before it's time…every time."

"Grandma?"

"Sleep, my Layla. Tomorrow, the world will be all new."

CHAPTER FORTY-FIVE
CRICKET

I SAT ON THE FRONT PORCH OF LAYLA'S CABIN patting the little dog's head and waiting for the sun to rise. I could smell the daylight in the air, but the sky was still dark blue. The last stars twinkled in the night's sky. At this point, my neck hurt from looking back and forth from the back of the property toward the gate. No Tristan. No Layla. I hadn't felt this on edge since the day Daddy turned the juice on to his refurbished tilt-a-whirl. I remembered how the red, blue, and yellow lights sparkled back to life. The ride slowly sprung forward and started her smooth turns, around and around again, the cars moving like fine ladies dancing across a ballroom dance floor. This anticipation…well, who knew what lay on the other side.

The front door opened. I turned to see Vella coming out. Frankie rose and wagged his tail.

"It's too early," she told me, settling onto the porch swing beside me. "Amelia is still sleeping."

"But couldn't Tristan and the others get through? I mean, would Amelia's spell—I guess that's what you call it—keep him out as well?"

"I hope so," Vella said then.

"You hope so? Why?"

"Because if it can keep Tristan out, it can keep everything

else out too."

I sighed and looked back toward the gate. "You think they're going to make it?"

"Yes," Vella said assuredly.

"You think it or you know it?"

"I know it."

"Cards?"

"No, I just know."

"Well, I suppose that will have to be good enough for now. Darius ever fall asleep?" I asked. Darius had been pacing the house all night worrying about Chase. Despite Ariel's best efforts to get him to sleep, he was still sitting drowsy-eyed at the kitchen table when I'd gone outside.

Vella laughed. "He's in the chair…snoring."

We were both quiet then, watching the clouds drift by. Slowly, the sky filled with more and more light. After a while, a light purple haze filled the skyline as the first rays of light began to filter over the mountains.

I nearly jumped out of my skin when the door opened once more. This time, Amelia was standing there. The poor girl looked like she was a mess of nerves.

"Anything?" she asked.

"No. Only quiet," Vella told her.

"Logan and the others?" she asked.

"Nothing."

Amelia nodded. "Well, I guess it's time," she said then crossed the yard toward the gate.

Vella and I followed behind her.

Amelia took a deep breath, closed her eyes, and then set her hands together, rubbing her palms in circles. She raised her hands before her and abruptly lowered them.

The air seemed to shiver.

Amelia then went to the gate and opened it, stepping outside.

There was no one there.

"Maybe...maybe it didn't work. Maybe the enchantment is still going," she said, looking back at Vella.

"They aren't there?" I asked, joining Amelia on the other side of the fence. I looked down the long driveway toward the road. There was no one. "Vella? Did it work? Can you tell?"

"It worked."

"But they aren't here," Amelia said pensively.

"No, maybe not yet, but they will come."

"Are you sure it worked, Vella?" I asked.

"Yes."

"But how do—"

"Because *they* are here," she said, pointing behind her.

I looked around Vella to see Tristan, Logan, Madame Knightly, and a man and woman I didn't know walking toward the house. You didn't have to be psychic to tell me the pair were important people. The air around them seemed to hold them in regard.

Amelia and I came back inside, closing the gate behind us. We crossed the lawn to meet the others.

"Amelia, Cricket, Vella, this is my daughter, Peryn and her husband, Obryn. They are the king and queen of our people," Madame Knightly said.

Amelia and Vella inclined their heads politely.

"Pleased to meet you," I said, sticking out my hand.

Obryn smiled politely and shook my hand. "You must be Cricket."

I looked up at Tristan who winked at me.

"I am," I said, letting go of his hand.

"Where is Layla?" Peryn asked.

"Not back yet," Vella said.

Peryn frowned.

The door to the house opened and a sleepy-looking Darius, along with Ariel, came out. It wasn't long afterward that everyone else was up and eager to see what was happening. Beatrice, Elle, Brian, Brianna, and Frenchie and her girls soon joined us.

"Where's Layla and the others?" Elle asked.

"Not back just yet," I replied.

Darius looked at Ariel who nodded and the two of them bounded down the steps. "We'll go look for them. They might be in trouble," Darius said.

"Or worse," Ariel added.

"No. Wait," Tristan said, lifting a hand.

We paused and listened. A moment later, we heard an engine headed our direction. Darius and Ariel ran to the fence and opened it, letting Tom drive through.

"Oh, thank the Goddess," Amelia whispered under her breath.

Tom parked the truck, and the others got out. Everyone was there, and no one looked hurt.

"What happened? Everyone okay?" I asked. Layla looked pale and rattled, but the others looked all right for the most part.

"The vampires were there," Will said. "They set a trap."

"We got lucky," Tom said. "Layla and Zoey discovered them before they discovered us. They're gone, at least for now."

"They are a dying race now, just like mankind," Peryn said.

"Peryn," Layla said softly, coming closer.

"You've done your best, Layla. And you're home now."

"The kitsune...what will happen now?" Layla asked.

"Their people are divided, but we've brokered a peace for

you, for now," Tristan said.

"So long as we no longer interfere," Peryn added.

"And just what does that mean?" I asked, looking at Tristan.

"It means they will cease their fight against you, but you must remain on your own from now on."

"Meaning, they won't attack us anymore, just leave the dead world to destroy us," Chase said sharply.

"Tristan, you didn't agree to something like that, did you?" I asked.

But the look on Tristan's face told me he had.

"There was no choice. Your revenge against them was justified, but their rulers are dead. That isn't something they accept lightly."

"So you mean to say, so long as you just let us live or die, now that you went ahead and saved us in the first place, they'll be fine with that."

"They don't expect us to live," Layla said, her words dark and hard. "They've condemned us to death, just like they wanted from the start. And you've agreed to this?" she asked Peryn.

I stared at Tristan. I could barely believe what I was hearing.

"No," Logan said. "Our people have agreed to remove ourselves from the fight. But we haven't condemned you," he said then looked to Madame Knightly who nodded.

"There is a way for you to keep yourselves safe," Madame Knightly said, turning to Amelia. "From the night walkers, the undead, and the kitsune."

"How?" Elle asked.

"I…I have to separate the worlds," Amelia whispered, her eyes wide.

Madame Knightly nodded.

I looked at Tristan. If they had promised to remove themselves from the battle, did that mean the man I loved was about to leave me?

CHAPTER FORTY-SIX

LAYLA

"TIME TO GO," PERYN SAID.

Madame Knightly set her hand on Amelia's shoulder and whispered in her ear.

Amelia nodded then kissed Madame Knightly on the cheek.

The matriarch squeezed the girl's shoulder, kissed her on the forehead, then turned and joined Peryn.

I turned to face Peryn one last time. If Amelia could really do it, could really drop the veil between this world and the world of the undead, then we could live on. We'd become like the faeries, creatures of legend. We'd belong to our own Land of the Young, a land beyond the veil of the dead world.

"Layla," Peryn said, "you have lost much, and I am sorry for it. But look what you have done," she said, gesturing to the others who were gathered around to watch, and lend their support to Amelia. Everyone was gathered, that is, except Tristan and Cricket who were in the middle of a heated argument. "It will be up to you to begin anew."

"How?"

Peryn smiled and leaned in toward me. "You're not the only ones we sheltered from the undead. Find the others. Build a better life. A new world awaits, and it needs you."

I cast a glance at Tristan who was now holding Cricket

against his chest.

"Amelia will need you too. Lend her your strength," Madame Knightly said. "And please watch over her."

I nodded to Madame Knightly. "I will. I promise," I said then turned back to Peryn. "Thank you…for everything. I wish I'd done better," I said. I felt the weight of my failure hanging on me.

"Let go and move forward," Peryn said, gently touching my chin. "Let go. It's time to see something new."

Peryn, Obryn, and Madame Knightly turned and walked away, disappearing into the ether before my very eyes.

CHAPTER FORTY-SEVEN
CRICKET

"SO, WHEN WERE YOU GOING TO TELL ME you are going to leave me all alone," I half-yelled at Tristan even before we were out of earshot of the others.

"Peryn and Obryn have commanded me to return—"

"So, after all this, you're going to leave me just like that?"

"Cricket," Tristan whispered, pulling me to his chest, holding me so tight I couldn't have struggled to get away no matter how angry I was. "Cricket. I told them I won't leave you. I'm not going back."

My heart leapt into my throat. I leaned back and looked at him. "Wh-what?"

"They forbid me to stay, but they've known me many years. I told them I'm not going back and that's that."

"And...and what did they say?" I asked, dashing my tears off my cheeks.

"They told me to look after Logan," he said.

I looked back at Logan who stood beside Amelia. I understood Tristan's words then. Logan, it seemed, wasn't going anywhere either.

"Tristan?"

"I love you. I promised I would do everything I could to keep you safe. I didn't mean just against zombies, unseelie, and vampires. I'll keep you safe against splinters, colds, banged shins, and everything else. I love you. I'll never leave your side."

"I love you too," I whispered then fell into his arms, joy spinning around and around in my chest like a tilt-a-whirl.

CHAPTER FORTY-EIGHT

AMELIA

"YOU CAN DO THIS," LOGAN WHISPERED THEN STEPPED BACK.

I cast a glance back at Vella.

She nodded to me.

I closed my eyes. This was much more, much bigger, than anything I had ever tried before. But if magic was real, if all the things I had ever seen, ever felt, all the things that had been beyond everyone else's vision were real, then I could do this.

Opening my eyes, I looked out at the woods. I remembered how the light used to look. Everything had become so dark, all the life in our world muted by the pall of death that hung over everything. I fixed my eyes on the space in front of me and willed myself to see the life inside the trees, the deep well of raw energy that lived within. I willed myself to see the energy that flowed up from the ground, from the roots, from deep within the living planet. I felt the great pool of life inside Mother Earth, hidden below the surface, buried by so much garbage—the hatred, the rage, the disconnect, the pollution—and the dead. I could feel them too. They were like blisters on the world, symptoms of the rot that had destroyed us. I reached out and felt the energy of the people gathered around me. I felt the love between Tristan and Cricket, the joy coming from Kira and Susan as they dared to hope, and life I hadn't known even existed, a tiny heart beating inside Ariel's womb. There was so much goodness here. I felt Layla's strength and Vella's sense of the otherworld which resonated with mine.

I put all my thought, all my strength, all my energy and focus on the world of color and light.

All the good.

All the joy.

No evil.

No darkness.

Just love.

With thanks, I pray thee.

And with a scream, I ripped the world in two.

CHAPTER FORTY-NINE

LAYLA

THE SHRIEK AMELIA LET OUT STRUCK ME TO MY VERY CORE.

There was a strange shift, as if the entire world had shuddered. The earth moved under my feet, and an odd gust of wind washed over us, rolling with tremendous force. But the wind was warm and perfumed with such sweet scents, the likes of which I'd smelled only on a warm spring day deep in the woods. The smell was fresh, and earthy, and alive. I staggered, barely staying on my feet, and then the moment passed.

Suddenly everything was so bright. It was like sunshine after a storm had passed. Sunlight glimmered on the green leaves overhead, making them sparkle. The sky was a vivid periwinkle blue. Everything and everyone around me seemed to shimmer with brilliant light. It was like someone had turned up the colors on the world.

"Beautiful," I whispered.

I felt a warm hand slip into mine.

Kellimore moved close to me. He was looking at the sky. His blue eyes glimmered like brilliant topaz stones, his cheeks a sweet rosy color. And I felt a sweetness radiating from deep within him.

A hazy memory, drowned by vodka, came to mind. It was like watching a scene from a depressing movie, a sad, drunk girl confessing what she was better off leaving unsaid. But now, in this bright air, something felt different. A flicker came to life in my heart.

The little dog Cricket had found barked happily.

"Look, Mommy," Kira said. "Amelia tore the world."

"What did you say?" Frenchie asked.

"See?" Kira said, pointing up toward the sunny sky. "She tore the bad part away. Don't you feel it? Only the happy part is left."

I gently squeezed Kellimore's hand then turned and looked at all the joyful faces around me. We were finally safe.

What a thing to see.

EPILOGUE

KIRA

I SLIPPED MY BOW ONTO MY BACK and dropped the rabbit into the game sack. Two rabbits. That should be good enough. I looked up at the sky, feeling the warm rays of light on my face. It was summer again. The pink pine needles below my feet made a soft cushion, the trees perfuming the wind with their sharp scent. I turned and headed back toward town, following the trail which ran along the river's edge back to Hamletville. I walked down Brighton Street toward the elementary school.

When I got close, I caught the scent of wood smoke and roasting meat. In the distance, I heard laughter. I wasn't late. Soon, I spotted them. In what had once been the playground, people had gathered for the midday meal.

"Kira," Layla called, crossing the grass to meet me.

I smiled at her, my chest filling with love and gratitude at the mere sight of her. "Two rabbits," I told her, handing her the game bag.

Layla laughed. "Is this why you're late?"

"I'm not late," I said, my eyes scanning the parking lot. Well, maybe I was a little late. Will's truck was parked and looked ready to go. He stood talking with Jason, Marcus, and Courtney, who were also ready to head out.

Layla raised an eyebrow at me.

"Okay, I'm late, but they say pregnant women have cravings for a reason. I couldn't let our baby girl go without," I said then, setting my hand on Layla's swollen stomach.

"Or baby boy," Layla said with a laugh. "Kell is convinced it's a boy. But anyway, thank you. Now come on, I have something for you, too."

"Oh cool," I said, catching sight of Cricket. "She got it working." For months Cricket and Andrew, a former engineer who'd found his way to Hamletville, had been working on a clockwork device. They'd dismantled the playground roundabout and affixed it with a seat that rotated in quick turns while someone cranked a lever. Cricket's and Tristan's daughter, Clementine, laughed wildly while she held on for dear life.

"I don't think I've seen her look that happy since the day Clementine was born," Layla said then led me to a picnic table. On top of the table was a bundled package. "Here," she said, handing it to me.

"What is it?" I asked.

She smiled. "Just open it."

I slowly unbundled the parcel. Inside, I found a sword. But it was not just any sword. I recognized it from Layla's collection as one of the swords she'd had with her since the beginning, or the end, depending on how you looked at it.

"Scimitar," Layla said, lifting the blade.

"But Layla, I can't accept this."

"Of course you can," she said then slipped a belted scabbard around my waist. "You're my best student, and you'll need a good sword with you if you're going out there."

"It's safe though. You know that, right?" I said, smiling softly at her.

"I know, but just in case. Never know. Maybe you'll get into a tangle with a tiger."

"A tiger?"

"All those zoo animals had to go somewhere, right?"

I pulled her into a hug, giggling as I struggled to move around her large belly. "Thank you, Layla."

"You're welcome."

"There you are," Susan called. "Will was looking for you."

I let go of Layla and turned to my sister. "Yeah, I know. I'm ready. Where are Mom and Tom?"

"Inside. They're coming out now."

"Kira," another voice called. "Safe travels," Amelia said, joining us.

"Thanks. So, we're headed west?" I asked Amelia.

She nodded. "Vella and I gave the map to Will."

"And what are you expecting we'll find?" I asked leadingly. At this point, those of us who still went out pretty much knew that whenever Amelia and Vella had a hunch about a place, we'd come back with something…or someone.

"I guess you'll see when you get there."

"All right, all right."

I turned to see my mother and Tom come outside. "I better go say goodbye. Don't have that baby before I get back."

Layla smiled at me then looked across the field at Kellimore who was turning a deer on the spit. It was as if Kellimore felt her gaze. He turned and smiled at her, a look so full of love that it made me blush. Someday, I was going to find a love like that.

"Safe travels, Kira," Amelia said.

"Thank you," I said then turned to Layla. "Thank you again," I said, patting the sword.

She nodded. "See you soon."

"Okay, let's go," I said, hooking my arm with my sister's.

"A sword?" Susan asked.

I pulled the blade from the scabbard and gazed at it. It glimmered in the bright sunlight, reflecting the colorful world around me. I realized then how lucky I was. Unlike Layla, I wasn't heading out to fight the undead, vampires, kitsune, or anything else. I was headed out in search of something better: hope.

THANK YOU

I hope you enjoyed *The Harvesting Series.* Might I ask a small favor? Would you consider posting a review? It helps me out a lot, making the book more visible to potential new readers.

Even though we are saying goodbye to Layla, Cricket, Vella, and Amelia, I'd love it if you kept in touch. Please join my mailing list, and I'll let you know about all my upcoming releases.

Thank you for taking this ride with me. Starting the zombie apocalypse is a lot easier than ending it. I hope you've enjoyed the ride. I know I did. Much love and many thanks!

Little Layla by Heather Ainsley

ACKNOWLEDGEMENTS

With many thanks to Becky Stephens, Lindsay Galloway, Kerry Hynds, Naomi Clewett, Carrie L. Wells, Mark Fisher and Electromagnetic Press, Erin Hayes, the Airship Stargazer Ground Crew, the Blazing Indie Collective, and my beloved family.

Also, my thanks goes out to all the bloggers and readers who've supported this series. Thank you so much for taking a chance on my quirky little spin on the zpoc.

ABOUT THE AUTHOR

Melanie Karsak is the author of *The Airship Racing Chronicles*, *The Harvesting Series*, and *The Celtic Blood Series*. A steampunk connoisseur, zombie whisperer, and heir to the iron throne, the author currently lives in Florida with her husband and two children. She is an Instructor of English at Eastern Florida State College.

Keep in touch with the author online.

http://www.melaniekarsak.com/
https://www.facebook.com/AuthorMelanieKarsak/
https://twitter.com/melaniekarsak
https://www.pinterest.com/melaniekarsak/

FIND MY BOOKS ON AMAZON.COM

62941623R00154

Made in the USA
Lexington, KY
22 April 2017